ANOMALY ON CERKA

QUANTUM LEGENDS – BOOK 1

BY ANDREW DOBELL
& M. D. COOPER

Just in Time (JIT) & Beta Readers

Chad Burroughs
Gareth Banks
James Brandon

Version 1.0.0

Cover Art by Andrew Dobell
Editing by Jen McDonnell, Bird's Eye Books

TABLE OF CONTENTS

FOREWORD

Thank you for picking up this book.

Firstly, let me say I am incredibly proud of this book. Working with Michael on this has been a tonne of fun right from the start, and I can't thank him enough for joining me on this crazy ride.

The genesis of this collaboration and the Quantum Legends series was an interesting one, and led to the book you're now reading. Quantum Legends was born from the BOB's Bar anthology. In that book, my character, Amanda, met Tanis for the first time, and they got on really well. At the end of that book, Amanda mentioned to Tanis that if she could find a way to visit her universe, she would.

It was a throwaway line, but it was the genesis of an idea. So, after BOB's Bar, I got talking to Michael, and I did some thinking about how it would work in story terms, and the plan was born. Shortly after that, I asked Barry Hutchison if he'd be interested in this too. He also agreed, and the series idea was born.

It's taken several months to get to this point, but it's been totally worth it.

I really hope you enjoy this book.

Thank you.

Andrew Dobell

CONTINUITY

If you have picked this book up and you're wondering where it fits into the larger stories of Star Magi or Aeon 14, hopefully this will clear up any confusion.

Star Magi
Anomaly on Cerka slots in between book 1 and book 2 of the Star Magi Series, so the reading order looks like this:

Maiden Voyage: Star Magi Saga Prequel
Star Magi: Star Magi Saga book 1
***Anomaly on Cerka*: Quantum Legends book 1**
Magi Nexus: Star Magi Saga book 2

Within Aeon 14, the book slots into the second season of the Perseus Gate series, between books 3 and 4. If you're reading the Orion War series, then it fits in between books 3 and 4 of that series.

Perseus Gate Season 2
A Surreptitious Rescue of Friends and Foes: P.G. Book 3
***Anomaly on Cerka*: Quantum Legends book 1**
A Victory and a Crushing Defeat: Perseus Gate book 4

Orion War
Destiny Lost: Orion War Book 1
New Caanan: Orion War Book 2
Orion Rising: Orion War Book 3
***Anomaly on Cerka*: Quantum Legends book 1**
The Scipio Alliance: Orion War Book 4

PREVIOUSLY IN THE MAGI SAGA…

Amanda-Jane Page is a Magus from Earth, having lived for over a thousand years, fighting the forces of darkness—powerful creatures known as Archons that were freed from Earth's Spirit Realm.

These creatures fled into the depths of space, and Amanda followed. There, she discovered and joined an ancient and advanced civilization of Magi living throughout the galaxy. Today, Amanda's self-appointed mission is to hunt down these Archons, and others who would destroy or enslave humanity.

During her adventures, Amanda traveled outside of her universe on two separate occasions and drew the attention of a multiverse-traveling Magus known only as Void.

She met with Amanda, and Void told her that she is one of a very small number of Magi who can use their power to cross into other universes. Void also informed her that some of these Magi use this ability for their own personal gain.

Amanda pledged her support to Void, who said that when the time came, she would contact Amanda for help.

That time has come…

PREVIOUSLY IN AEON 14...

Sabrina and her crew have spent over a month in the Virginis System, which they visited twenty years prior. It was once independent, but after Sabrina set about liberating its AIs, it became a founding member of an alliance of star systems known as the League of Sentients.

The principles of the LoS were not compatible with the nearby Hegemony of Worlds, and as that empire began an expansionist surge, it surrounded Virginis, and ultimately attacked.

Despite facing a far superior foe, the people of Virginis held off the aggressors—though they fell back to the inner system, ceding everything beyond 4 AU from the star.

This was the state Virginis was in when *Sabrina* and crew arrived, only to find themselves immediately embroiled in a coup attempt on Cerka Station—the system's capital. They were able to stop the coup, but the system was still far from secure.

Jessica contacted Tanis, who agreed to send a number of destroyers to the system to aid in its defense. However, the people of New Canaan were still recovering from the attacks on their own system, and many of the ships are incomplete, meant to function more as a deterrent than an actual defense.

In the wake of those events, Jessica and her team got wind that some old friends were in trouble on Chittering Hawk Station—well within the AST-controlled region. Despite the threat, they launched a rescue operation, freeing many AIs, humans, and a number of captured ships from the enemy.

From there, they returned to Cerka to await the ships from New Canaan. Things seem to have settled down, and the enemy forces in the outer system have not made any moves to take the inner worlds and stations.

It seems like the perfect time for a relaxing night out....

SABRINA'S CREW

Amavia – Ship's Engineer (ISF Commander)
Cheeky – Pilot
Iris – AI formerly embedded in Jessica (ISF Commander)
Jessica Keller – Ship's Captain (Brigadier General)
Misha – The cook
Sabrina – Ship's AI
Trevor – Supercargo and muscle
Usef – ISF Marine (Colonel)
Jinx – An AI recently liberated by *Sabrina's* cew.

NOTE: When *Sabrina* is italicized, it refers to the ship, but if Sabrina is not italicized, it refers to the AI. Yes, this would be much simpler if the ship and AI did not share the same name, but you try telling that to Sabrina!

Just so you stay on her good side, never call the ship "**the** *Sabrina*"; it really gets on her last synthetic neuron.

STAR MAGI CHARACTERS

Amanda-Jane Page – Arch Magus, *Arkady*'s Captain.
Void – Arch Magus & Multiverse Traveler
Rane Ormond – Ormond Dynasty Heiress
Samhain – Amanda's Familiar

CELEBRATION

STELLAR DATE: 05.10.8948 (Adjusted Years)
LOCATION: *Sabrina*, Cerka Station
REGION: Mullens, Virginis System, LoS Space

Jessica flipped a microdrone ahead of herself as she walked down *Sabrina*'s port-side cargo deck passageway, and spun it to aim its optics at her.

An image of her progression appeared on her HUD, and she watched the long, blue dress slide across her body, pleased with the way her left thigh peeked out of the slit—which doubled as a useful way to grab the lightwand that was hidden within her thigh.

A deep sigh of satisfaction escaped her lips, pleasure from both the recharging session she'd just completed in *Sabrina*'s rear observation lounge, and also from the knowledge that she and Cheeky would finally be able to resume the outing they'd been on when the call from Chittering Hawk had interrupted them.

Granted, since it was the tail end of Cerka's second shift, a lot of shops were closing, which meant she and Cheeky would simply have to enjoy the *other* type of celebrating one was prone to during the evening on a well populated station: food, dancing, and sampling the local alcoholic concoctions.

<You ready yet, Cheeks?> Jessica reached out to her friend and ship's pilot over the Link.

<Almost, just making a final decision,> Cheeky replied with a drawn-out sigh.

Jessica sent a laugh over the mental connection. *<Do you need a hand?>*

<No,> Cheeky snorted, and the impression that the other woman was sticking out her tongue came into Jessica's mind. *<I think that every so often, I should be able to get dressed without a consult from you.>*

<OK, I'll just go through some reports while I wait. I should be able to get through a few…dozen while you make up your mind.>

<Hey, Jess, seriously. That's…uh…probably an accurate estimation, thanks.>

A happy smile graced Jessica's lips. Everything was right in the universe. The team was aboard *Sabrina,* kicking ass in outer space. They'd just bearded an AST fleet, rescued some old and new friends, and on top of it all, her best friend Cheeky was back in the land of the living.

"I really *do* need a night out," Jessica muttered aloud as she reached the airlock.

"Don't we all," said a tired voice, and she turned to see a

man standing outside the open airlock, a sheet of plas in his hand.

"Dammit, buddy," Jessica muttered. "Don't do that to a person, I coulda killed you."

The man wore a shipsuit with a holo-logo hovering over each shoulder that read 'Tora Livestock – Cerka's Finest'. His eyes slid down Jessica's body, and a small smile appeared on his lips.

"Not sure where you'd hide a weapon under that dress—uh, er…sorry, ma'am."

Jessica suspected that the man—whose Link ident tagged him as 'Pauly'—had just realized he was speaking to a brigadier general, the same general who had saved his station two weeks prior. She nodded wordlessly for him to continue.

"Sorry…" he said again. "I saw you when you gave the speech last week at the president's press briefing. You looked…a lot different then."

"Really?" Jessica asked with a look of scorn. "I've not seen a lot of glowing purple women on your station. Plus," she held up her hands, and electricity arced between them "I don't really need to carry weapons."

Pauly was blushing furiously at that point and nodded quickly. "Sorry, General. I meant no offense."

Jessica scowled at the man for a moment longer before giving him a solemn wink and then chuckling.

"Relax, Pauly. Do you think I'd wear a dress like this and *not* want people to look at me? I'd ogle me too, if I were you."

Pauly gave her a guarded look and then nodded slowly. "Umm…of course, ma'am."

"OK, what do you have there?" Jessica asked, knowing that nothing she said would get the man to lighten up at this point.

A definite downside to being a renowned general. I wonder how Tanis copes? No, nevermind, I doubt she even notices.

"Two crates of chickens, a full feeding system, pens, the works."

Jessica glanced up at the overhead. "You were serious, Sabrina? You ordered chickens?"

<*Yup!*> the ship's AI said brightly. <*Now that I'm sometimes using mobile frames, I want to try tending animals. It should be fun. Plus, it will save having to listen to Misha complain whenever Trevor eats a few dozen eggs in one sitting.*>

"What can I say?" Trevor asked as he ambled down the passageway toward Jessica. "I'm a growing boy. I need protein."

"You gonna tend to the chickens when Sabrina gets bored?" Jessica asked him, taking in the sight of her massive husband in a rather form-fitting shipsuit.

Trevor snorted and shook his head. "Right. Like that's going to happen. I'll just cook them all. Fresh roasted chicken for dinner!"

<Trevor!> Sabrina exclaimed in their minds. *<You're **not** going to kill and cook my chickens!>*

"Well who's going to look after them after it's not new and novel anymore?" Trevor asked. "You can't just have a bot do it. Animals need real interaction."

<Easy,> Sabrina said, a grin appearing in their minds. *<I'll make Misha do it. He's kinda like my little bot.>*

Jessica couldn't help but laugh at the AI's matter-of-fact statement. Sabrina certainly did enjoy ordering Misha around—though it was always in good fun. She knew Misha didn't mind it either. He had a soft spot for the starship's AI.

"So…I just need someone's token on this delivery," Pauly said, still standing in the airlock. "It's been a long shift, and I have my own party—with my friends, pizza and beer—to get to."

Trevor planted a kiss on Jessica's temple as he ambled past. "OK, let's have a look. We might need to take it around to the main bay's doors."

Pauly backed out of the airlock, disappearing around the

corner. Trevor stopped at the lock's entrance and shook his head as he regarded something to his left.

"Fuck. That's a shit ton of chickens."

<I want to make sure we have lots of eggs.>

"Do you want to start up a side-business selling them, too?"

<Oh! That would be cool!>

"OK, Pauly my boy, we definitely need to take this stuff around to the main bay doors. We can't get those crates through the corridors on the port side."

"Have fun, hon," Jessica called out as Trevor disappeared around the corner.

A deep laugh came in response, and his voice echoed back through the airlock, "Nobody here but us chickens!"

"Oh stars," Iris muttered as she approached. "And so the chicken jokes begin."

Jessica glanced at the AI and smiled to see her 'other half' approaching in a silver dress that perfectly matched her own.

Iris had spent twenty years embedded in Jessica's mind—roughly the maximum for a human-AI pairing. The AI had been very young when their partnership had started, and had come to identify strongly with Jessica's highly modified figure as being her 'body'.

Consequently, when she'd had to leave Jessica, she opted to get her own body that mirrored—quite literally, since it was a gleaming silver replica of Jessica's—the body she'd been in for the past few decades.

At first it had bothered Jessica, but she'd come to accept that Iris really loved looking like her, and it meant a lot to the AI to have a familiar shell, so she didn't contest it.

Over the past few weeks, she'd even come to enjoy the sight of her silver doppelganger—something enhanced by the new three-way relationship Jessica and Trevor had entered into with the AI.

Of course, all that didn't stop Jessica from needling Iris over her choice.

"Face it, Iris, if you could, you'd just push my brain out of this body and take over."

The AI paused and gave Jessica a measuring look. "Hmmm…I'd never considered that before. It wouldn't be too hard to pull off, either, but I think I'll pass. Now that your alien microbes have completely suffused your body, they create a rather high risk of internal electrical discharge. That's a bit much for me."

"Huh…you did just fine for a decade. Though your core is very well insulated. Stars, what am I saying? *No,* you cannot kick me out of my own body. Not even for a chrome dome like yours."

Iris shook out her long, silver hair. "My dome's not chrome. It's *lustrous*."

The sound of heels snapping against the deck came from behind them, and Jessica turned to see Cheeky approaching. "If you two are done dancing around how attracted to your collective self you are, can we get going? The night's a-wasting."

Jessica smiled to see that Cheeky had gone back to the basics: a pair of white heels with a white bikini.

"Kicking it old-school?"

"You bet!" Cheeky winked at the pair. "You two look great, by the way."

"Thanks," Iris said, giving a small shimmy. "You know, this is my inaugural 'out on the town' event with my own body."

"Oh ho!" Cheeky exclaimed with a broad smile as she linked arms with Jessica and Iris. "Let's make it a good one!"

"Hold up, Cheeks," Iris said, stopping the pilot short. "Jinx is coming, too."

"Oh?" Cheeky freed their arms and peered over her shoulder. "I thought she was uncertain about venturing out on

Cerka."

"I told her if she doesn't come with us, I'm going to drag her kicking and screaming off the ship," Iris replied. "She can't hide here forever."

"I'm not hiding," Jinx said as the AI strode around the corner in the silver and blue mobile frame Sabrina had loaned her. "I'm just…acclimating."

Jessica covered her mouth to hide a laugh. "You're also naked, Jinx."

The AI's eyes widened as she took in the three women in front of her and then looked down at herself. "Damn…am I supposed to get dressed to go out? I mean…this isn't an organic body like you have, Cheeky. Am I supposed to cover it in cloth? That seems…inefficient."

"Ignore Jessica," Cheeky said as she held out a hand for Jinx. "She's an alien now, what does she know?"

"I'm not an alien," Jessica grumbled. "I'm more human than you are, Cheeky."

"Sure, Jess, whatever you say. The fact that your body's been converted into a purple alien power plant is hawt, kay? Own it."

Jessica shrugged. "I guess I might as well. It's not like you're ever going to lay off on the alien jokes."

"See?" Cheeky laughed as she clasped Jinx's hand and pushed Iris and then Jessica into the airlock ahead of her. "My plan is working. Just a couple of alien and AI girls heading out onto the station for some dancing, drinking, and if we're lucky…."

"There's luck involved?" Jinx asked with a worried look on her flowmetal features. "I don't think I'm very lucky."

Jessica leaned back and whispered loudly to the AI, "Sex. Cheeky's talking about having sex."

"Do AIs *have* sex?" Jinx asked. "I barely understand having a physical body. Attraction and intimacy are totally foreign to me."

A boisterous laugh burst from Cheeky's lips, and she turned to walk backwards in her towering heels, skipping past Iris to the front of the group.

"You know what they say, Jinx…."

"Ummm…I do?"

Cheeky winked and then turned to face forward once more, adding an extra sashay to her saunter. "I wasn't always an AI."

Jinx's brow furrowed. "But I was, so…"

"Jinx!" Cheeky called out over her shoulder. "Stop overthinking it!"

*****

"Cerka's lame," Cheeky complained as the four women sat on a pair of sofas at the edge of Club Noir's dance floor. "Why did we save such a lame station?"

She and Iris had just returned from a session of gyrating that had only brought three others to the floor, so when the song ended, everyone had returned to their seats.

"Pretty sure that we don't save places based on the merits of their nighttime entertainment," Jessica replied as she took a sip from her third nova bomb…or perhaps it was her fourth.

"Maybe we should add that to a checklist of things we think about before we put our lives on the line," the pilot said, a sulky expression settling on her normally cheerful features. "I mean…we're heroes! I should get at least *some* action for that."

"I think it's *because* we're heroes," Iris suggested. "Maybe we're intimidating."

Jessica looked over the group and nodded slowly as she assessed her companions. "You might be right. I mean, look at us…we look like ancient goddesses who have come down to smite or save humanity. Love us and despair and all that."

Jinx leaned closer to Iris. "I can't tell if she's kidding. Is she kidding?"

Iris laughed and shook her head, silvery hair dancing across her shoulders. "Stars, I have no idea, and I've spent most of my life in that purple noggin of hers."

"I think she's drunk," Jinx said as she peered at Jessica's eyes. "But it's hard to tell—her eyes are glowing, and I can barely see her pupils."

"See?" Jessica shrugged. "Goddesses."

"She's drunk," Cheeky confirmed.

"And still human!"

Iris patted Jessica's cheek lightly. "Only because she wants to be. It's a breeze for her to clear out her blood. Heck, I still have access to do it remotely."

"Don't you dare!" Jessica ordered, grabbing Iris's hand by the wrist. "I've been stone-cold sober since we left Orion Space, and I plan to break that streak with a vengeance tonight."

"OK, well, either way, we're going to continue this somewhere else," Cheeky said as she rose. "I've settled up our tab and left a tip. There's a place on one of the lower rings called 'The Smash and Grab' that I think will be more our speed."

The other three women rose and followed Cheeky out of Club Noir. As they walked toward the door, Jessica kept an eye on a hooded man in a nearby sofa alcove. He was surrounded by women, but had hardly paid any attention to them all night.

He had, however, spent a lot of time staring at Cheeky, rather lewdly.

She checked his ident and saw that he was a merchant who was stuck in the inner Virginis system, burning credits while he waited for the stalemate with the AST to end.

She considered chastising the man, but though she could read his ident, he didn't seem to have a Link channel to talk on. Ahead, Cheeky had already reached the club's exit, and Jessica picked up the pace to reach the rest of the group.

At the door, Jessica took a moment to mentally congratulate herself for making it without even a wobble.

<I see that smirk,> Iris said privately. *<You're not as steady as you think.>*

<Steady enough. Let me enjoy this. I've got some weighty decisions to make soon, and I plan to blow them off as long as possible.>

Iris sent a compassionate smile into Jessica's mind as the four ambled down the concourse, Cheeky explaining to Jinx how to spot the best shops that carried authentic local goods.

<*You mean decisions like whether or not we leave after Tanis sends that destroyer squadron?*> the AI asked.

<*I mean whether or not we use it,*> Jessica elaborated.

<*But most of them are just hulls.*>

<*AST doesn't know that. And from what we saw out at Chittering Hawk, we're clearly working against the B-team here.*>

Iris sent a feeling of agreement. <*And if we push them away and secure Virginis, what then?*>

<*Then we move on as planned, following our path from twenty years ago. Next stop is Aldebaran…well, plus a few hops along the way.*>

<*And Virginis? What if the AST comes back?*>

<*Well, that's the question, isn't it?*>

Iris didn't reply, and Jessica pushed the weighty thoughts from her mind as they reached a maglev platform that would take them to the station's central spire.

The group chatted idly as they entered the rear car and took a group of seats facing one another. Several passengers came by to thank them for stopping the coup on Cerka two weeks prior, and for rescuing friends from Chittering Hawk.

Eventually, the maglev dropped them off at one of the station spire's central hubs, and the group moved to a lift, taking it down to Ring Three's level, where the 'Smash and Grab' was located.

Once there, Jinx asked if they could walk along the spoke that led from the spire to the ring, and the others agreed, taking a broad concourse with a clear overhead that let in the system's brilliant light, setting Jessica's skin ablaze.

"I have to say," Jinx mused as they walked past a series of shops that all sold flower arrangements—and by the signs on display, were all in fierce competition with one another. "Downtime for organics is a lot different than it is for AIs. You just do mindless things."

"Mindless?" Cheeky asked. "I suppose we do. It's just nice to be relaxed and not under pressure."

"Don't you get that while sleeping?" Jinx asked.

"Sort of," Cheeky replied. "But here, we're building the bonds of friendship as well. Making and strengthening relationships."

Iris snorted. "Somewhere in there is at least one euphemism."

"Just one?" Jessica asked.

"Hey!" Cheeky said with an indignant squeak. "I'm more than just se—Shit...what was that?"

The four women froze, and Cheeky passed a marker across

the link, highlighting a corridor on their right that ran past a pair of mod shops.

<*What is it?*> Jessica asked.

<*I heard a pulse shot down that passage.*>

Cheeky was closest, and her body was the best that Earnest Redding could make, so Jessica didn't doubt the woman's hearing.

<*You armed, Cheeks?*> Iris asked as a pulse emitter emerged from the palm of her hand.

<*Of course I am,*> the pilot replied as she pulled a lightwand from her thigh. <*I've danced this number before.*>

Jessica felt her head clear and glanced at Iris. <*I could have done that. Besides, a fight while buzzed can be fun.*>

<*I hope you're kidding, Jess. You were more than 'buzzed',*> Iris replied.

<*OK...probably. But I still protest you using my nano to convert my alcohol system back to blood.*>

Iris glanced over her shoulder as she followed Cheeky down the side passage. <*So change your codes.*>

Jessica didn't reply, other than to shoot Iris a narrow-eyed look as she followed after.

She knew she *should* change her root codes. There was no reason to allow Iris so much latitude with her body when the

AI no longer resided within it.

Maybe later.

The passage Cheeky was inching down was dimly lit, but none of the four women had any trouble seeing in it. Cheeky reached the corner, and a feed from her drones appeared on their shared channel. Jessica tapped into it and saw that a quartet of people wearing dark clothing were huddled around a door that led into an auxiliary comm node.

<Well, that doesn't look good,> Cheeky commented. *<I can see a body on the floor beyond them. Must be station security.>*

<OK, let's pay them a visit,> Iris said, beginning to pull off her dress. Cheeky was already ahead of the AI, her body disappearing from view, only her floating bikini giving away her location. Then that hit the floor, and she was gone.

Jessica glanced down at her dress, debating whether it was worth it or not for her to join the others, while Jinx—who wasn't wearing anything to begin with—strode past her and disappeared from view.

<OK, well, let's at least switch to tactical,> Jessica said as she flipped their shared channel to a combat net.

<Think we need it for some common crooks?> Iris asked as she finally divested herself of her clothing and disappeared from sight.

<You're the one that made me sober. Now you have General Jessica, not Party Jessica.>

<Touché.>

Jessica decided to remain clothed, and leant against the bulkhead while watching the other three women's progress on the feeds.

The four targets got the door open, and two disappeared inside as Cheeky reached them. One of the remaining crooks, a stocky woman, walked to the fallen station security officer and grabbed him by the ankles.

"Jal, help me with this dick," she said to the man standing on the far side of the door.

"With his dick? I don't think so. You're on your own, Mary."

"Fuck you, Jal. Dude weighs a ton. Grab his arms."

The man pushed himself off the wall and ambled toward the other robber, only to trip and fall, barely catching himself on his hands before his face hit the deck.

"What the hell?" he muttered, glancing back to see that there was nothing he could have tripped on.

Mary was chortling as she looked down at her fallen comrade. "You're such a tool, Jal. Get up already."

The man didn't have a chance to reply before something hit

his face, snapping his head to the side as blood sprayed from his nose.

Mary opened her mouth to cry out, but then gasped and reached for her throat, eyes bulging as she clawed at an invisible hand.

Then something hit her head, and she was out.

<*Wow, regular people are weak,*> Jinx commented as Mary fell to the ground.

<*The cop's still alive,*> Iris said. <*But he's got internal bleeding. I've dropped some mednano on him, but I think the pulse blast ruptured a few things that shouldn't rupture. Let's wrap this up fast so we can call for medical help.*>

Jessica walked around the corner, moving toward the downed CPS officer, while the markers for the other three women showed them moving through the door after the other two thieves.

She pinned the feeds from her team to the side of her HUD as she knelt next to the cop.

"Officer Dale, this is not your night."

She dropped more nano on him and set the pulse emitter in her left palm to emit a gentle sonar wave as she ran it over his abdomen. Iris's assessment had been accurate; the man's stomach, spleen, liver, and lower intestine had all split open, turning his insides into a toxic soup.

She searched his uniform, finding nothing.

Sheesh, where's a canister of biofoam when you need it?

<We're clear,> Iris called from inside the comm node chamber. *<They were trying to breach it, looking for access codes to docking supply systems.>*

<That's interesting. Think they were trying to steal fuel or something? I've called their emergency services with an officer down. Why don't you and Cheeky go get dressed? Jinx can cover those two.>

<C'mon, Jess. I kinda want to have them come to and see me naked and unarmed, standing over them. That would be a riot.>

Jessica leaned around the corner and looked into the chamber to see Cheeky doing just that.

"Cheeky, seriously, this station has laws about nudity."

"Fiiiiiine."

* * * * *

"Any idea what they were going for?" Detective Alla asked Jessica as she watched the medics secure her downed comrade to a grav pad.

"Nothing beyond the systems they were trying to breach. I

guess we could have let them get further to see what they were after, but your buddy Dale here needed someone to put him back together before his insides dissolved."

Alla pursed her lips. "Dale shoulda known better than going down here alone. If these are the same dickheads we've been after for the past week, they're dangerous. Killed more than a few people on their break-ins."

"Damn," Jessica muttered. "You'd think with all the shit they've been through, people would have had enough of violence."

The detective nodded. "Most have. But there are always some who see this as an opportunity for the big score."

A dozen memories from her days back in the TBI on High Terra came to Jessica, and she nodded soberly. "I know that song all too well." She clapped a hand on the detective's shoulder. "You need anything, let me know. We're happy to testify against these asshats."

"I'll take you up—"

Detective Alla stopped midsentence, and her eyes narrowed, locking on Jessica's.

"What is it?"

"I just got pinged about a woman we picked up…she's looking for someone from the ISF. That's your military, right?"

Jessica nodded. "Yeah, sure is. My crew roster is public.... This woman after one of mine?"

"No...she wants someone named Tanis Richards."

VOID SHIFTING

EARTH DATE: 07.18.2017

LOCATION: Sol Prime, Nexus Space, 200 AU from Sol

REGION: Another Universe

Essentia surged around Amanda, and she sensed the powerful, reality-warping magic of the Arch Magus Void reach out and shift them both instantaneously from her room inside the Sol Prime space station to somewhere else.

Void was a Magus, like Amanda, but an ancient one who had the rare ability to cross between universes, and she'd been interested in recruiting Amanda to her cause.

Having agreed to help her, Amanda had not seen Void again since their initial meeting a year before. Until now.

They stood in a large intersection of corridors in what she could only assume was another space station or spaceship. Void floated nearby, her chrome body wreathed in endlessly moving, fractal-like energy that reminded Amanda of mercury. She could see her own distorted reflection in Void's skin. Amanda's long, bright red hair fell over her shoulders, contrasting against her glossy white and grey bodysuit.

Through her Aetheric senses, Amanda knew they were still in her own universe, but they were a long way from Sol.

"Jaysus," she cursed. "I am sensing this right, aren't I? We've just Ported halfway across the galaxy?"

"That is correct," Void answered, her voice soft and melodious, with a curious pitching effect to it. "We're in Crux space, close to the galactic core."

"Crux space? You can Port that far?"

Void smiled. "I can, and so can you."

"Yeah, right," Amanda chuckled disbelievingly, and looked around her.

Corridors led off in several directions. The air had that sterile, artificial taste to it common on stations, and she could hear the soft hum of the station's systems working away in the background. Most Riven humans wouldn't be able to detect such subtleties, but Amanda's enhanced senses were far from those of an average human.

"I'm not that powerful, yet..." Amanda answered Void.

"You're more powerful and capable than you think. Distance is an illusion, Amanda. All things are connected. Linked. You're limited by your very human reliance on your perception of three dimensions, but there are many more dimensions, and the quantum reality is such that concepts of distance and time are not what we humans think they are."

"You're telling me that I can teleport clear across the galaxy?"

"When you're ready, you can Port to other galaxies, but that is not why I brought you here."

"No?"

Void slowly shook her head from side to side, her silvery hair floating around her head as if it were in water. "No. You already know about the concept of other universes, other realities. You have already passed outside of this reality twice."

Amanda nodded. "BOB's Bar, and then to meet my mother."

"Correct. I myself have traveled far beyond this reality, and you will too, but we're not the only ones capable of this. There are others, from other realities, who have visited this one. One such breach happened only recently, and began right here," Void explained.

There were cargo crates piled around, but nothing terribly noteworthy, Amanda noticed.

"What happened?" she asked.

"A group of people from outside this reality shifted in and aided a man called Jaiden. The man was part of the crew of a ship named the *Void Star*. He had discovered some very sensitive information about the movement of a certain group of Void Dragons, and was attempting to return to his ship. These people from another universe aided Jaiden, who was able to return to his ship and inform his captain about the dragons' movements. Kora passed this information onto Valerya, and you know the rest."

"Jaiden was the one who discovered that the Void Dragons were heading to Earth, then?"

"Correct."

"Is he alive?"

"He is," Void answered.

"How do you know all this?"

"I'm very sensitive to beings passing into and out of whatever reality I am in—it's how I found you. When I sensed this breach, I investigated."

"So who were these travelers?"

"Mercenaries. A team led by someone called Jon Hunter. They appeared to be pawns in the plans of a greater power. I can show you, if you'd like?"

"Of course," Amanda said.

She felt Void's Magic reach out to her mind, and allowed the Arch Magus to reach into her head. She knew she could trust her, mainly because her mother, Sophia, did. Suddenly, images and knowledge flooded her mind, and she had perfect recollection of the events that had happened to Jaiden.

She took a moment to think them through and get them straightened out in her mind before she smirked and looked back up at Void.

"A cocky fellow, isn't he," Amanda commented. "So, what does this all mean? Is it important somehow?" she said, looking over at the section of decking where this mister Hunter had killed a young Nomad Magus with his Magical sword.

"I'm unsure. Maybe it means nothing, but, it's another breach of the multiverse with a connection to you. You're not a typical Magus, Amanda…that much we both know."

Amanda nodded as she closed her eyes and returned to the events surrounding Jaiden's escape, including his flight from the station aboard Jon's ship, the *Gunbus*, – which had also crossed over into this universe with Jon – and its fight with a Void Dragon before more weirdness happened. A pair of Magic users appeared, who finally got Jaiden to his ship.

"I need to thank Jaiden sometime," Amanda commented.

"He doesn't have perfect recollection of the events that happened to him here—another effect of transuniversal travel that you have also experienced."

Amanda nodded again, remembering the trouble she'd had remembering what had happened to her during her visit to BOB's Bar.

"So, you said you had some missions for me?"

"Indeed, I do," Void answered. "Within this reality, I am not the only Magus with the ability to cross between universes. There are others. One group, who call themselves Reavers, have taken this power and turned it into an operation for their personal gain. They visit other universes, hunt for anything that might be of value, and steal it, bringing it back to this one. They also trade items, polluting universes with tech that shouldn't be there, and recruit team members. As you can probably imagine, this could potentially be very dangerous."

Amanda understood. While many things, such as a coffee cup, could cross over quite harmlessly, technology or Magic could be disruptive or downright lethal, were it to be brought back and fall into the wrong hands. They could change the course of wars and worse.

"Such as Jon's ship, the one that Jaiden took a trip on," Amanda answered.

"Indeed, the *Gunbus* had extrauniversal tech on it," Void

agreed.

"Tell me what you need me to do."

"A Reaver has crossed over into a universe that you have a link to. The universe that Tanis Richards is a part of."

"Tanis? From BOB's Bar? Oh, wow."

"Correct."

"Alright, count me in. Are you going to send me there?"

"No need. You can cross over yourself."

"Excuse me?"

"Amanda, you're not like most Magi, and you easily meet the requirements to make such a trip. Usually, only un-sundered Arch Magi have the potential to cross between universes, but your extra-universal heritage works in your favor, making it that much easier for you. In addition, you have a link to that universe already, meaning it's unlikely you will get lost."

"Lost?" Amanda asked, curious.

"The multiverse is huge, vast, possibly infinite, and if you're not careful, it can be all too easy to lose your way. Magi have left this universe in the past, never to return."

"That's not good."

"I have faith in you, Amanda. You will not get lost."

Amanda blinked, feeling her cheeks begin to burn. "Thank

you…" she said, feeling a little embarrassed by Void's belief in her.

To say she had her doubts that she could make such a trip would be an understatement. She did, however, trust Void.

"So, how do I do this?" Amanda asked after a moment's pause to take in what she had just been told.

"It's no different from the usual way you Port from place to place. Focus on where you want to be and impose your will on the veil of Essentia. A word of warning, though: this will likely be exhausting for you, not least because it's your first attempt."

Amanda nodded once. "I understand."

Void's usually neutral face smiled, an expression that looked a little odd on her chrome face. "Then please, go ahead."

"So, I should focus on Tanis?"

"Only enough to focus your mind on her universe. Instead, focus more on the mission I gave you. You have enough details to get you to the right area."

Amanda took a deep breath. "Alright, here we go." She closed her eyes.

Focusing her thoughts, Amanda pulled on the Magical energy of Essentia that was everywhere, all around her, and cleared her mind. As she gathered the energy to her, she first focused on Tanis, and then on the universe she was within. As the image of the tall, blonde woman solidified in her mind, she added in thoughts about the Reaver, someone from her universe who was already there, where she wanted to be, and began to impose her will on the extra-dimensional energy that was now rushing through her.

She forced her wishes to become reality, picturing herself in that universe. Her Magic surged as light flashed behind her eyes, and an intense feeling of dislocation washed over her. She collapsed and landed on a hard floor, knowing she was no longer in her own world.

She'd crossed realities.

Feeling drained, like she'd just run several marathons back to back, Amanda only wanted to curl up and go to sleep.

"Stars! Who's that?" said a gruff voice close by.

Amanda blinked her eyes open and looked up. She realized she was sitting in the middle of some kind of alleyway. The ground was dirty and covered in scraps of litter.

"Of course," she muttered. "Where else would I appear?" Alleyways seemed to be a recurring location in her life.

She shook her head to clear her mind as she pushed herself up to her feet.

"I said who the hell are you?"

Amanda heard the unmistakable click of a weapon a little too close to her head for comfort.

She looked up to see a man pointing the business end of a handgun at her.

"Well, I'm not in Kansas anymore," she said to herself, noticing that the buildings around her stretched up to a metal overhead with pipes and cables running over it. Her Aetheric senses were still a little fuzzy from the trip, but she quickly realized she was aboard a space station of some kind.

"What?" the man asked.

Amanda noticed movement behind him. Further up the way, three thugs were beating up a victim against the wall.

"What's going on up there? Who's the babe?" one of them called.

Amanda felt her eyebrows creep up her forehead at the comment and had a feeling she knew where this was going. She checked her Aegis, the Magical force field that hugged her skin; it was still there and going strong. She was also relieved to note that Essentia still flowed all around her, visible in her Aetheric Sight.

"No idea," the man next to her answered his friend.

"Kill her, then, we don't want no witnesses."

Amanda wasn't sure if she could get away with using Magic in this world, but it was becoming clear that she might need to defend herself.

"Shame. Sorry, Red," the man said, and squeezed the trigger.

The slug thrower fired, and a round slammed into her Aegis, ricocheting off into the nearby wall.

Amanda smiled at him.

The man looked shocked.

"What the hell!" yelled one of his companions further up the alleyway. "I meant do it *quietly*. Stars, now we're going to have station security on our asses."

She wasn't sure how much the man in front of her heard, though, as Amanda wasted no time in retaliating.

Sweeping her hand, she hit his wrist with her fist, feeling and hearing his bones crack as his pistol flew from his grip. She followed it up with a swift kick to his groin, making him bend forward, where his face met her knee. Blood splattered over her white and grey bodysuit as his nose exploded.

The man coughed, spluttered, and made several unintelligible noises as he shuffled back, nearly tripping as he went. Amanda followed and delivered a kick that hit him like a battering ram, her enhanced strength making short work of him. He flew back ten meters, hit the floor close to his companions, and lay still.

The remaining three thugs stopped attacking their victim and turned to face Amanda. Their previous target slumped to the ground and looked up to see what was happening.

"You're going to regret that," one of the aggressors said, and they all pulled out weapons—ranging from small, snub-nosed blasters to huge, formidable-looking hand cannons.

"You think?" Amanda asked.

The lead man didn't answer other than to sneer at her, and then all three opened fire, sending bullets, and in one case, an electron beam, at her. The blasts hit her Aegis and either stopped dead or rebounded harmlessly.

She wanted to end this quickly, but she also didn't want to kill these idiots. With a thought, she focused her will and hit the three of them with a powerful Kinetic punch.

They were knocked off their feet, landing on the ground with solid-sounding thuds.

The victim's eyes went as wide as plates as he watched the confrontation, only for his gaze to be drawn to something behind her.

Crap, she thought.

She'd not been concentrating, and the mental fog from

crossing into this universe was still interfering with her senses, meaning she'd missed the additional people rushing into the alleyway behind her.

"CPS! Hands up," a female voice barked at her.

Amanda relaxed her stance and took a deep breath, held it, and let it go slowly. It wasn't the ending to this little fight that she'd wanted, but maybe it would work itself out.

Slowly, she raised her hands.

"Get on your knees," the voice continued.

Amanda did as she was asked and listened closely. Her Aetheric senses felt five humans approaching behind her, wearing body armor and carrying some serious weaponry. One of them stepped up to her and grabbed her wrists to bind them.

The man that the thugs had first been attacking got up and started to make his way over to them, dripping blood.

"Sir, please stay where you are," one of the men behind her ordered.

"But she saved me. She's not the one you need to arrest. You need to take these guys," he said, waving toward the thugs.

"Don't worry, we will," the CPS officer said as three others moved forward to cuff the men indicated.

The guard finished binding her hands and moved around into her field of view.

"Is that right?" the officer asked Amanda, referring to the other mans comments. "What have you got to say for yourself?"

Amanda looked up at the woman with a slight smile on her face. "I want to see Admiral Tanis Richards of the ISF," she said, remembering the logo on the outfit Tanis had worn when she'd first met her.

"Who?"

A VISITOR

STELLAR DATE: 05.10.8948 (Adjusted Years)

LOCATION: En route to CPS Station, Cerka Station

REGION: Mullens, Virginis System, LoS Space

"So, who's Tanis Richards?" Jinx asked as the four women followed Detective Alla to the police station where the suspect was being held.

"She's the leader of our people," Iris explained. "The Governor of New Canaan and also the head of our military."

Jinx cocked her head, regarding Iris with a look of suspicion. "Seems a bit totalitarian."

"Yeah," Jessica said, laughing as she considered how outsiders would see Tanis. "But now that the military effort is taking more of her time, she's stepping away from the governorship."

Jinx seemed unsatisfied by the answer. "OK, but New Canaan is three thousand light years from here. Who would show up at Virginis expecting to be able to talk to her?"

"It's not super surprising," Cheeky said. "Well, I mean, that people are looking for her. After what she did in Bollam's

World...."

"Wait!" Jinx interjected. "I learned about that back when I was a nav AI. We were fed the details of a battle with the *Intrepid.*"

"That's the one," Jessica nodded. "We all fought at Bollam's. Tanis led our forces."

"Which is why people might seek her out. Since we're kinda representing the Intrepid Space Force, I guess it kinda makes sense that someone wanting to talk to Tanis would come here to us."

"No," Jessica shook her head. "It really doesn't. The AST has this system under blockade, which means anyone looking for Tanis has been here for weeks, which means they would *have* to know she's not with us."

Cheeky shrugged. "Well, I dunno...maybe this woman's been living under a rock somewhere. I know it's hard to believe—and I'm only half being sarcastic here—but we're actually *not* the center of the universe."

"That's because there is no center of the universe," Jessica countered.

"That's not exactly true," Iris replied, glancing at Jessica and then shaking her head. "Oh, nevermind, you're just being argumentative. I don't know why I didn't pick up on that."

"Me either," Jessica replied.

Detective Alla glanced over her shoulder at the four women, and shook her head. "Core, the four of you talk like a gaggle of teenagers."

"Really?" Cheeky asked brightly. "Thanks! I think that's what keeps us so youthful."

"I don't think she meant it as a compliment," Jinx said in a quiet voice.

Cheeky shrugged. "Doesn't matter, I'm going to take it as one anyway."

Alla laughed. "Honestly? I really have no idea how I meant it."

As the detective spoke, she turned onto a large thoroughfare that ran down the station's central spire, and gestured to the CPS station. It was set into the right side of the concourse, covering five levels of the sweep, and people were flowing in and out of the entrance like it was a hopping club.

"Is it…always that busy?" Jessica asked.

"No." Dala shook her head. "Only since you got here."

Cheeky winced. "Sorry."

"Not your fault." The detective waited for a lull in station car traffic and then led the group across the concourse. "Mostly it's people trying to resolve damages from rioting and fighting—so first we have to figure out who broke what and then pass the reports on to the insurance carriers. Since a lot of people have fled Cerka, and a lot of refugees have shown up, we're seeing a wave of break-ins."

"Like the one we just saw," Jessica added.

"Well…more petty theft. And to top it all off, everyone who isn't pissed that something precious to them was broken is out partying every night, happy to be alive, so we're dealing with people smashed out of their minds."

Examining the composition of the crowd moving in and out of the CPS station, Jessica could see that, at present, there appeared to be more of the former types than the latter.

"Well, hopefully we can take this woman off your hands and give you one less thing to worry about," Iris said.

Alla gave the gleaming silver AI a long look. "Well, you'll try, but you four strike me as the type to get into the thick of things at every turn."

Cheeky gasped and placed a hand on her chest. "Why, I do believe you…have us totally made."

Detective Alla bellowed for the crowd to "Make a hole," and finally led the four women into the station.

It didn't surprise Jessica that the interior was a doubling down of the mass of people on the exterior. People were crowded in everywhere, trying to reach the front desk, explaining that they'd only been "drinking for a day or two," and pleading their case to disinterested officers.

<*Stars…reminds me of the bad old days,*> she said on the group's private channel.

<*Oh?*> Jinx asked. <*You were a police officer once?*>

<*Don't listen to her,*> Iris shot Jessica a knowing look. <*Jess was never a beat cop. She was a federal agent back at Terra.*>

<*Right, for a population in the hundreds of billions. Trust me. We had all kinds, and whenever there was a pan-system football game, our offices looked pretty much like this for a week or two.*>

Alla led them through the CPS station, using her glower as a weapon to drive a wedge into the crush of people and AI frames.

They came to a rear corridor that only had a few pockets of people—mostly CPS officers—talking in hushed tones. Most of the groups were standing outside of doors that Jessica assumed led into interrogation rooms.

At the end of the hall was a room with a heavy carbon-fiber door, guarded by two heavily-armed soldiers—Virginis Defense Force, not CPS cops—standing on either side.

"VDF?" Jessica asked. "Has Admiral Hera taken an interest in our visitor?"

"No," Alla shook her head. "Once I let them know I was bringing you in, the captain decided not to push it up the ladder. The VDF just has a few 'toons rotating through to give us a hand."

"Oh?" Iris asked. "Where are the rest of them?"

Alla sighed. "Trying to deal with a group of punks who are racing modded cars through residential corridors."

"Shit," Jessica muttered. "And here we were having a night out."

The detective cast her an understanding glance. "Trust me, if half what I hear is true, you and yours pull your weight. I don't begrudge you a night off."

"Me either!" Cheeky exclaimed.

They stopped at the door, and Alla looked to the corporal standing on the right side. "Any issues?"

"No, ma'am," the man said. "She hasn't moved a muscle. Cool as a cucumber in there—so far as we can tell, at least."

Alla turned to Jessica. "I guess our sensor systems in the room can't really get much of a read on her. She shows up fine on optical and IR, but try as they might, the most the sensors can do is pick up skin temp and blood pressure. She gives off almost no other EM. It looks like she has no mods."

"That's interesting," Jessica mused. "What's the protocol?"

"Well, there's not really room enough in there for a whole party. Why don't you and I both go in and see what she has to say?"

Jessica glanced back at the other three women with her. Cheeky was leaning up against the wall, eyeing the corporal, while Iris said, "I'm tapping your optics."

"Oh, I want in on that," Jinx added.

"I'll put the feed on our channel," Jessica replied with a shake of her head. "Busybodies."

"Jess," Iris deadpanned. "We're AIs. We are doing half a dozen things right now and still feel bored. I just solved two cases that detectives were working on as we walked through the main room back there."

"I helped on one," Jinx added. "The one guy had the ship's engine burn profile all wrong in his statement. Stank to high heaven."

"Shit," Alla chortled. "You two want a job?"

"Hell no," Iris added. "Keeping Jess's purple hiney attached to her body is pretty much a full-time job as it is. But we'll help while we're here."

Iris waved to Jinx, and the two AIs walked down the passage to where a group of detectives were standing next to a door, shaking their heads.

Cheeky glanced at them, and then back at the corporal. "Well, I got your Link ident. You ping me when you're free, kay?"

The man laughed. "I'm already trying to swap shifts."

"Cheeky!" Jessica admonished her pilot, smiling to show she was only half serious.

"What? That club was a bust, but I'll be damned if I don't end tonight without one date arranged," Cheeky replied with a wink.

The pilot ambled down the corridor to join Iris and Jinx, while Alla gave a bemused sigh. "Quite the crew you run with."

"More like family than crew," Jessica replied. "Most of us have been together for two decades."

Alla laughed. "Then you're not family, because any family *I* know would have murdered one another after just five years on a ship that small."

Jessica only laughed, but she stilled her voice as the detective opened the door.

Even before it was open wide enough to see the occupant, a voice called out from within, "What's the craic?"

Jessica had already pushed a nanocloud into the room and had been watching the woman for the last minute. Even so, she took a moment to take her in once she and Alla entered.

The first thing about her—and it was impossible to ignore—was her long, bright red hair. If it wasn't plain for Jessica to see that the woman was unmodded, she would have thought it was glowing.

<*Maybe you're not the only one around here rocking bioluminescence,*> Iris commented.

<*Hush, I'm looking stern,*> Jessica replied.

She continued to take in the woman, noting her green eyes and slightly pointed chin. Her body was clad in a white shipsuit that Jessica made a note to scan carefully so she could replicate it at some point.

Detective Alla was right. So far as Jessica could tell, there was no EM coming from the woman's head, but her shipsuit possessed some tech—though it wasn't from anywhere around the Virginis System.

However, what was most interesting was that the woman sat leaning back in her chair, one leg crossed over the other, with her hands resting on her thighs. That in and of itself wasn't strange, it was the open pair of binders sitting on the table before her that made the woman's pose interesting.

"Inside joke," Jessica finally said in reply to the woman's question.

"Corporal, why isn't this woman in binders?" the detective called out through the still slightly open door.

He popped his head back in. "But she… I… Oh," he replied, seeing the redhead without them on.

She raised her hands in the air and wiggled them about with a playful smile on her face. "Tadaa," she sang.

"Don't worry about it, close the door," Jessica said, glancing at the corporal.

"Of course," he replied with a perplexed expression on his face as he complied.

"So," Jessica continued, about to ask her first question, when the woman spoke up, interrupting her.

"You're *very* purple," she said with an eyebrow raised.

Jessica eyed the suspect for a moment before continuing. "The information I have says that your name is Amanda-Jane Page, and you're looking for Tanis Richards."

Amanda rose and stretched out her hand, smiling brightly. "That I am, Miss…?"

Jessica regarded the redhead's hand for a moment then shrugged and reached out to shake it. Worse came to worst, she could fire her electron beam and blow off the strange woman's hand should she try anything.

"General Keller," Jessica said, then nodded to her right.

"And that's Detective Alla."

Amanda gave Jessica's hand a single shake and then reached out for Alla's. The detective reluctantly shook, and then pulled out her chair, sitting down, Jessica and Amanda following suit.

"Well…" Amanda said as she settled back into her prior pose. "A detective and a general! I'm certainly moving in the right direction."

"What do you know about Admiral Richards?" Jessica asked.

"Admiral? Well, I suppose she might have been, she did have a few stars on her uniform…. Well, whatever, we shared a drink and some stories a while back."

"And when was that?" Jessica asked.

"Oh…" Amanda tapped a finger on her chin. "I don't know, about a year ago?"

Jessica's brow rose in skepticism. "You were in New Canaan a year ago?"

Amanda shook her head. "New Canaan? In Connecticut? No, I was in New York, on Earth… mostly."

<Is she just playing me?> Jessica asked.

Cheeky laughed. *<Beats me, but I'd sure like to play with her. You know what they say about redheads.>*

Iris groaned. *<It's clearly not natural, Cheeky.>*

<And that matters why?>

"OK, Amanda," Detective Alla's voice was cool and emotionless. "Just tell us where you met Admiral Richards."

"To be sure. We met in BOB's Bar."

"Wait, whoa, what?" Jessica sputtered. "You know Bob? *The* Bob?"

This time it was Amanda who fixed Jessica with a curious stare. "Well, there're a lot of Bobs around, what do you mean by *the* Bob? This Bob was a little different, admittedly, him being a robot an' all, but nothing that special."

"Weird," Jessica muttered. "Though I guess it's a bit of a common name. So, where was this bar?"

Amanda pursed her lips. "You know…that's a really good question. I feel like that's something Tanis should be the one to share with you, though. You're not likely to buy it from me."

"Is that right?" Jessica glanced at Alla, who only shrugged in response.

<She must have heard Tanis's name from the Battle of Bollam's World, realized that our 'ISF' is named after the Intrepid, *and put two and two together,>* Iris surmised.

<Sure,> Jessica replied. *<But at Bollam's World, Tanis held the rank of general, not admiral.>* She realized her skin had begun to

glow as she became more frustrated, and tamped it back down as much as she could.

"You know, Tanis was able to do some rather impressive things with her modifications and nano, but she didn't glow."

Jessica smirked at the idea of Tanis glowing, but as much as Amanda seemed to have a fun sense of humor, this conversation wasn't going anywhere.

"No, she wouldn't. It's nothing like that." Jessica shook her head. "My body is suffused with an alien microbe that has the photosynthetic properties of chlorophyll and retinal. It absorbs light and gives off my lovely purple hue. I can also tap into it for energy if I need to."

"Alien?" Alla asked, her eyes growing wide.

"Don't worry, it's not something you can catch." Jessica leant forward and placed her hands on the table. "Sorry, detective, I don't think I can take this one off your hands. Hopefully we've been more help than trouble tonight, though."

Alla nodded. "You saved Dale's life and took a shot at Red here. We're in your debt."

"You're here with Cheeky, aren't you? The blonde in the fetching white bikini, standing out in the hall?" Amanda suddenly asked, a mischievous look twinkling in her eyes.

<*She could have heard me?*> Cheeky offered.

<*You were pretty chatty with the guard there,*> Iris confirmed.

<*They have some major soundproofing in this room,*> Jessica countered. <*And this woman has no mods. Also, she's knows you're blonde….*>

"Why don't you ask Cheeky about the time she and Tanis went out for some drinks on…what was it…the PetSil Mining Platform, or some such place?"

<*Cheeky?*> Jessica asked. *This is getting a little weird.*

<*Sure, yeah, we were there for a few days and went out. Not exactly a huge secret,*> the pilot replied.

<*But it's on the far side of the Hegemony.*> Iris added a feeling of doubt to her statement. <*Her knowing about that, and then showing up here just got a lot more suspicious.*>

"I know you're talking to her," Amanda said, peering intently at Jessica. "I can't yet figure out what you're saying, though—you have some impressive encryption algorithms."

<*OK, that's really weird,*> Cheeky said, sounding both nervous and intrigued.

"Ask her…" Amanda's voice trailed off for a moment, clearly in deep thought. "Ask her about what she was doing when Tanis was fighting that guy…shite…Maverick!" she said, snapping her fingers as she remembered. "Ask her what she was doing when Tanis was fighting Maverick with his plasma sword—well, he had the plasma sword at first, and she had a chair, if I remember it right."

<*Cheeky?*> Jessica asked. <*One, did that really happen, and two, how come you never told me?!*>

<*Holy shit…*> Cheeky's mental tone was a whisper. <*Tanis and I never told* ***anyone*** *about that. This woman is, like, a wizard!*>

<*OK…I know I grew up in a navigation computer, but I'm pretty sure wizards aren't real,*> Jinx corrected.

<*Whatever. It's hot. Like hotttt with extra 't's.*>

Jessica pursed her lips, boring her gaze into Amanda's eyes. <*We'll talk later about keeping secrets, Cheeky.*>

"Well?" Amanda asked.

<*I need some info, here, Cheeks,*> Jessica prompted.

<*I was…uhhh…sucking on someone's feet.*>

<*Cheeky! In the middle of battle?*> Iris exclaimed.

<*I was the distraction!*>

"Did she just tell you she was sucking on someone's feet?" Amanda asked. "I recall Tanis saying something like, 'she had half this guy's foot in her mouth', or something along those lines."

<*I have so many questions, Cheeky,*> Jessica said, trying not to laugh at the mental image of Tanis in a pitched battle while

Cheeky had half a foot in her mouth.

Some jokes were going to come from that one.

<OK…I don't remember all the specifics, but yes, it sounds like she knows about that…night out.>

"She corroborates your story," Jessica finally replied to Amanda.

"That's good, it would have been a real shame if Tanis had made that up. So, is there any way you can contact Tanis? I need to talk to her."

"We have a way," Jessica allowed, suddenly deciding that whatever this woman was up to, it would be far better to get her away from here and onto *Sabrina*. They could get her into a stasis pod if things got really strange.

"Great! How do we do it?"

"We have to go to our ship," Jessica replied, and glanced at Detective Alla. "Looks like I'm taking this one off your hands after all."

<You realize you don't need to go to the ship to use the QuanComm,> Cheeky said.

<Yeah,> Jessica replied. *<But I think it's best if we continue this conversation in a more controlled environment.>*

Alla took a second to reply to Jessica. "Stars, General Keller…I don't know if I'm envious of your life, or terrified."

"I don't see why you can't be both." Jessica rose and gestured to the cuffs, looking at their new guest. "Any chance I can get you to put those on?"

Amanda frowned. "Why?"

"Appearances," Jessica replied, flicking her eyes to the detective.

"Is that really necessary? I'm no threat to you, and I promise to be good. Guide's honor," the redhead replied with a mock salute.

<*Oh, she's going to fit right in,*> Cheeky commented.

Jessica rolled her eyes. "Fine. Follow me."

"Love the dress by the way, hope I didn't interrupt your evening. I can't wait to see your ship."

FRIENDS OF A FRIEND

STELLAR DATE: 05.10.8948 (Adjusted Years)

LOCATION: *Sabrina*, Cerka Station

REGION: Mullens, Virginis System, LoS Space

Amanda watched the purple woman leave the room, and moved to follow before looking at the binders on the table and smiling to herself.

She picked them up and fell into step behind Jessica—a pretty woman, if a little strange looking with her lilac skin and intense purple hair, all of which seemed to glow. Like everyone else she'd seen so far, she was also heavily modified, with all kinds of artificial implants and augmentations, including nano machines that surged through her body and bloodstream. It was fascinating to watched through her Aetheric Sight.

Jessica might not be Tanis, but Amanda was pleased to find that she was now at least in the company of some of Tanis's friends, including Cheeky out in the corridor. She'd been watching the blonde through a second set of senses she'd conjured out there, and the woman seemed to live up to the impression that Tanis had given of her through her story back in BOB's Bar.

Stepping out, Amanda smiled up at the guard who'd handcuffed her, and offered him the cuffs.

"Thanks, but they really didn't match my outfit, and they're seriously uncomfortable," she said sweetly, and dropped the cuffs into his hands.

"Uh, thanks," he said, looking slightly dumbfounded.

"No problem," Amanda replied and followed Detective Alla and Jessica into the corridor.

Alla watched her little chat with the guard and rolled her eyes at the interaction.

Looking ahead down the corridor, Amanda realized she still had her second set of senses active, giving her an additional view of the area that she didn't need, so she canceled the effect with a brief thought.

Walking through the passage, Amanda got a better look at Jessica's slinky, sparkly blue dress, which hugged her clearly modified form.

No one has a body shaped like that without having some work done.

Up ahead, Jessica's three companions were standing, talking to some of the officers. She spotted Cheeky right away, her blonde hair and bikini-clad body standing out like a sore thumb in the back corridor of the gritty law enforcement station.

Several of the officers were sending admiring glances at her, but Cheeky seemed to welcome it, smiling warmly at everyone around her.

Amanda noted the dress that Jessica's chrome clone wore, and felt sure she had interrupted a night out for the girls. *Hmm,* she thought, *I wonder if they'll pick up where they left off? I could do with a drink.*

The last woman looked shiny and metallic, the same way Jessica's clone did, and a quick look with her Aetheric Sight only confirmed what Amanda had suspected about these two—that they were AIs.

Jessica didn't say anything to Amanda as she led her down the corridor to the group, but Amanda could see the signals flitting between the purple woman and the others, suggesting that they were conversing through their encrypted neural Link, or whatever they called it here.

Having used her Magic to split her mind into several separate but linked parts—creating a hive mind—she assigned one of these to break the encryption in the Link that Jessica and the others were using.

They quickly said their goodbyes to the officers they had been speaking to and walked ahead of Jessica, threading through the press of people in the station.

Jessica glanced back at Amanda. "Keep up," she said, before turning back to follow her companions.

Amanda was curious to know more about these ladies, but she also wondered where Tanis was.

Is Tanis elsewhere in this system? Amanda wondered.

She'd gleaned the name of the system from some minds she'd delved into to get a better idea of where she was, but there were still lots of things she didn't know.

It took a good couple of minutes for the group to make their way outside, but as they left the police station and the crowds of people behind, she and Jessica quickly caught up with the others.

More signals flew between their minds as they regrouped, but it was the blonde who fell back to walk alongside Amanda.

"Hey. I'm Cheeky," she said, offering her hand in greeting.

Amanda took it.

"Hi, Cheeky, it's a pleasure to finally meet you."

"Likewise," she answered, with a smile that spoke of some naughty thoughts. "So, how do you know Tanis?"

"Well, it's a bit of a long story, and I think it might sound a little less crazy if it were to come from Tanis rather than myself. But I will say that we shared a drink or two and a few stories."

"And she told you what happened on PetSil with Maverick?"

Amanda smiled and nodded as the group continued to walk away from the CPS station. "Me, and the others that were there."

"...Others?" Cheeky asked, her voice a little squeaky.

"Not such a secret after all," Jessica cut in, raising her eyebrows at her friend.

"Sorry, I'm making it sound like Tanis is telling everyone about this, um...event...but there's more to it than that. I swear the only people who know about it, in this universe at least, are standing right here—apart from Tanis herself and the guy whose foot you sucked," Amanda winked.

Cheeky raised an eyebrow and then laughed. "Don't knock it till you try it. Besides, the distraction worked."

"I bet it did," Amanda answered. "And between you and me, I've sucked on a few toes myself. One of the hazards of a long life...You tend to try new things."

A beat passed, and after a flicker of a signal between

herself and Jessica, Cheeky shot the woman a look that was playful but also suggested that she didn't have much room to talk.

Amanda checked on the progress of the part of her mind she'd set to breaking through the encryption. It was close, but they had some serious security going. With a quick boost of Essentia and a working of Magic, Amanda enhanced that part of her mind, making it faster and more computer-like. She wanted to find out what these ladies were talking about. She'd have it in a moment.

She turned to the two gleaming, metallic figures who were walking with them. They smiled back at her.

"Hi, I'm Amanda," she said in greeting.

"Iris," the chrome clone of Jessica said.

"And I'm Jinx," the silver and blue one answered.

"Lovely to meet you. Look, I'm sorry for the secrecy," Amanda said, addressing them all. "But once I talk with Tanis, and she confirms who I am, this should all be a lot easier."

"That's fine, you'll be speaking to her soon, we just need to get to our ship," Jessica answered as she led them to a maglev station.

They waited in silence for a few minutes until a train arrived, and they boarded.

"Did I interrupt a night out?" Amanda asked as the train took off. She pointed to the dresses that Jessica and Iris were wearing.

"It was already interrupted," Iris answered, her tone sour.

"Not that there was a lot to interrupt," Cheeky added. "The LoS didn't pick this station as their capital because of its hoppin' third-shift."

"The night wasn't that much of a disaster." Jessica directed a tolerant smile at Cheeky. "Besides, you looked like you were getting on well with that guard."

"You're right," she answered, and then turned to Amanda. "Thanks for getting arrested," she said brightly.

"My pleasure," Amanda answered. "So why was it already interrupted?"

"We foiled a break-in," Jinx explained. "It was fun."

"A break in?" Amanda echoed.

"Before we go any further in this conversation," Jessica interrupted, "I think we need to have our chat with Tanis. No offense," she said to Amanda.

"None taken. I understand completely."

She could relate to Jessica's reticence in telling her too much; they really didn't know who she was or what her motives were. She decided to sit back and enjoy the rest of the journey, which included some more walking, as well as a lift ride.

Having spent time away from Earth in her home universe, and in the galactic community of the Magi, she'd seen some impressive sights, but there was something about being in a totally different universe that added a new sense of wonder to everything.

As they walked down a passage, she took in the people around her, admiring their clothing and body modifications, as well as the advanced technology on show. She was pleased to see that she didn't stand out too much in her fitted outfit and boots.

Eventually, after they turned onto a broad concourse with windows looking into space on their left side, Jessica turned to her.

"We're here now, *Sabrina* is just up ahead," she said. "You can see her out there." She pointed.

Amanda turned and looked out the windows to see a huge ship docked at the station. It was blue and silver with long, sweeping lines, and Amanda guessed it was maybe two hundred meters long. It looked quite majestic against the twinkling light of the stars beyond.

She nodded in approval. "Impressive ship."

"I'm sure she'll appreciate the sentiment," Jessica laughed.

She led her forward before turning left into the docking bay and moving toward the airlock. As they approached, a large man with muscles over his muscles ambled forward, his attention on Jessica.

"If I never see another chicken again, it will be too soon," he groaned.

"Don't be such a sourpuss, you were cooing over them too. You even named two of them," teased a voice coming from speakers beside the airlock.

"I don't know what you're talking about," he said and leant down to give Jessica a kiss. "Good night out?"

"Eventful," Jessica replied.

"I see we have more visitors," he said, looking at Amanda.

She raised her hand in a quick wave. "Hi," she said, and then offered it to him in greeting. "Amanda, lovely to meet you."

He took it, his hand swallowing hers as he gave it a firm shake. "Trevor," he answered.

"Amanda here was picked up by the CPS, says she knows Tanis and wants to speak with her," Jessica explained.

Trevor let go of Amanda's hand, and the smile dropped from his face. "And you took her at her word?"

"There was toe-sucking involved," Jessica answered him.

"What?"

"Look, I told you." Cheeky glowered at Jessica, hands on her hips. "I was the *distraction*. Tanis told me to do it."

Trevor opened his mouth to speak, shut it again, went to say something for a second time, and then paused once more before looking back at Jessica.

"What?" he repeated.

"Amanda here claims to know Tanis, and Tanis apparently told her a story that she and Cheeky had kept quiet about."

"And it involved toe-sucking?"

"More like half a foot," Amanda corrected.

"I'm so confused…and yet, not surprised," Trevor replied.

"I need to hear this story," the voice from the ship added.

"Tanis swore me to secrecy, but if she's telling strangers…" Cheeky paused for a moment, weighing her options. "What the hell, I'll share the whole story at dinner…or breakfast, whatever meal is next."

"And on that note. Hello, Amanda, I'm Sabrina," the female voice from the ship said.

Amanda's Aetheric sight penetrated the materials around her. She could see the energy within the ship and the presence of a sentient mind embedded deep within it.

"Lovely to make your acquaintance," Amanda said with a smile.

"You too!" Sabrina replied. "You're quite curious."

Amanda smirked at the ship's comments. "Thanks, I think."

"Right, let's get this over with," Jessica said. "Follow me."

As she led Amanda into the ship, Cheeky, Iris and Jinx followed, while Trevor went back to whatever work he'd been doing… Something about chickens, Amanda wasn't sure what though.

They didn't go far into the vessel before Jessica turned right and led them into a good-sized room. They'd entered through the only door, and the small pile of metal crates stacked in the corner suggested it was a cargo hold of some kind. Amanda turned to find Jessica with her arms crossed, looking confrontational again.

Amanda smiled. She didn't blame them. They didn't know her from Eve, and she seemed to have knowledge of events that few seemed to. They were right to be suspicious of her.

"Sabs, contact Tanis, and route the QC through to this hold."

"Sure thing, messaging her now."

Everyone stood silently, looking at Amanda while they

waited. She could see they were tense and ready for anything, but they really had nothing to fear from her.

Not that she would be able to convince them of that through words alone. No, for that she really needed Tanis.

It appeared that Jessica and the others on this ship were under her command; if Tanis remembered her and their meeting at BOB's Bar, then everything should fall into place. That was a big 'if', though…. The strange effect of the energies at the bar that had loosened their tongues and gotten them to talk about things they normally wouldn't had also had something of a fogging effect on the mind.

Still, Tanis was her one chance to get these people on her side so she could look into this station a little more. If what Void had told her was true, she should be in the vicinity of whoever it was that had crossed into this universe from her own, and it was up to her to find them and stop whatever it was they were doing.

A moment later, Sabrina's voice sounded from the speakers in the room. "OK, I'll transcribe anything you say. The QC network is text-only."

Amanda raised an eyebrow. "Is it? How will I know it's Tanis?"

"Well…" Jessica said, tapping a finger against her chin. "I

suppose you can ask her about something that happened at that mysterious bar that no one knows about, except all the people who seem to know about it."

As the purple woman spoke, a sentence appeared in the air between her and Amanda.

[Jessica. Ship's nearly ready.]

"That's a bit abrupt," Amanda commented.

"We skip words to keep usage low," Jessica explained, before the holodisplay hovering between them read, *[Have guest named Amanda. Knows you from Bob's Bar?]*

"Hi, Tanis. It's Amanda," she added. "Amanda-Jane Page. We met at BOB's Bar about a year ago—a year for me, at least—with Cal and Splurt and the others."

The words appeared in text form floating in the air, though pared down to just the essentials by Sabrina. *[Hi. – Amanda]*, appeared, below Jessica's explanation.

Amanda raised a single eyebrow in response.

[Shit. Amanda?] came Tanis's response. *[Seriously?]*

"Do you remember it? You told the story of your night out with Cheeky on the PetSil Station, where you encountered Maverick," Amanda replied as her words were transcribed again. *[Yes. I told Cheeky and Maverick story].*

[You told the Roswell story.]

"That's right," Amanda answered, beaming at Jessica, who had cocked her head and mouthed, 'Roswell?'

[Had half-wondered if the bar was a dream,] Tanis sent, then added, *[You come on your own?]*

"I did, yes. I just needed you to confirm to Jessica and her crew that I am who I say I am, and that we have indeed met before."

[Jessica, Amanda's legitimate. FYI, multiverse isn't a theory anymore.]

"Shit," Jessica muttered, shaking her head. "When were you going to share this?"

[Sometime. Amanda, why are you in Virginis?]

"I'm tracking down other travelers. I suspect they're on this station and I need to stop them. Where are you?"

[New Canaan, three thousand light years coreward. Damn, would have liked to see you.]

"Me too. Once I've finished up here, I might try to make the trip."

[Looking forward. Jessica, new mission, help Amanda.]

"Already planned on it," Jessica replied.

[Good.]

"She's gone," Sabrina told them.

Amanda smiled at the memory of the blonde woman she'd

met at the bar. It was good to hear from her again, even if it was just words and not her voice. She would dearly love to visit Tanis if she could. She knew that three thousand light years would be about a month's travel on an Aetheric craft—something she was more than capable of conjuring.

I'll think about it.

Looking over at Jessica and the others, she could see signals being sent between them, as they no doubt discussed what they had just heard. As she peered at those signals, the mind she had assigned to cracking the encryption suddenly made a breakthrough. She was quickly connected to their network and listening to their voices.

<*Did she say 'multiverse'?*> Iris was asking the group.

<*She did,*> Jessica answered, her eyes still fixed on Amanda.

~Hi, guys. Just figured out your encryption. Those were some serious defenses you had running there. I had to augment the mind I had assigned to hacking it quite a bit. Impressive.~

"What? How are you on the Link? You don't have any mods," Jessica asked.

<*So…hot!*> Cheeky commented, giving Amanda a lascivious look.

She winked back at the blonde, who smiled like a schoolgirl at the gesture. Then she frowned at Jessica. "You're right, I don't. Okay, so I have a lot to explain, and it's going to seem crazy, but you need to hear it if you're going to help me."

"Fair enough," Jessica answered, "and if Tanis trusts you, then I do too. Let's get everyone into the ship's galley so we can do this in one go, with alcohol and coffee on hand." She turned and walked out of the cargo hold. As Amanda followed the purple woman through the ship, Cheeky fell into step beside her.

"So, you're going to be around for a few days?"

Amanda glanced sideways at the pretty blonde, catching Cheeky giving her an appraising look. "Looks that way," she answered with a smile.

The woman was not being very subtle about her advances, but Amanda didn't mind. Cheeky was very pretty, reminding Amanda of a Californian blonde bombshell from Earth.

"Good…" Cheeky answered, looking like the cat who got the cream.

Amanda listened as Jessica sent out a call through the ship's net to the other crew, telling them where to meet.

After walking through several corridors and climbing a couple of ladders, they entered a room that was part futuristic ship's galley and part homely rustic family kitchen, with its scarred wooden table

The room had a good vibe, and she liked it immediately. She smiled at the five people she saw waiting inside as she walked in. She recognized Trevor from earlier, but there were two more men and two more women who gave her some curious looks as she followed Jessica in.

"Okay everyone, get comfortable," Jessica said, indicating that Amanda should find a place to sit.

She did, feeling watched as she moved around the table.

"So, you spoke with Tanis?" Trevor muttered to her as she passed.

"Yep, I did indeed," she answered, and slid into her seat, noticing Cheeky very purposely sitting opposite her, with a hungry grin on her face.

"So, what's going on?" Misha asked the group, glancing at Amanda as he spoke.

"Picking up more waifs and strays?" Usef muttered good-naturedly.

"I'm not a waif," Jinx commented.

"Right," Usef replied, his eyes twinkling as he looked from the AI to Amanda. "You're a stray. She's a waif."

Cheeky's eyes trailed down from Amanda's face to her chest. "Not that waifish, if you ask me."

"Cheeky, stop ogling our guest," one of the other women said, and Amanda recognized Sabrina's voice.

"Wait, are you the ship's AI?" Amanda asked.

"Uh huh," the woman nodded. "This is just a frame I use sometimes."

"When it's not being repaired after getting shot up," Trevor chuckled as he settled onto a stool near the counter.

"Get your head blown off *one time,*" Sabrina muttered.

"Alright, guys, let's focus. I want to properly introduce our new friend. This is Amanda, a friend of Tanis's who needs our help," Jessica said. "Though I don't quite follow what with."

Amanda noticed a more serious mood come over the group at the mention of Tanis's name. The woman clearly commanded a lot of respect from them.

"Amanda," Jessica continued, "before you explain what the hell's going on, let me introduce you to everyone. You've met Cheeky, Iris and Jinx. You've also met Trevor," she said.

The mountain of a man waved and nodded at her from where he stood beside Jessica.

"And of course, Sabrina," she said, pointing to an AI in a metallic frame. She had fins jutting from her body, like Jinx, but where Jinx had blue highlights, Sabrina's were red and gold.

"Pleasure to have you aboard," she said with a smile.

Jessica continued to point people out as she introduced them. "We also have our resident Marine, Usef, ship's engineer, Amavia, and the cook, Misha."

Usef touched two fingers to his brow in a salute, while Amavia and Misha nodded silently.

"Lovely to meet you all," Amanda said. "I'm keen to chat with you, but first, let me tell you a little bit about where I'm from and what I'm doing here. As Jessica said, my name's Amanda—Amanda-Jane Page. There's no way to say this without it sounding crazy, so, I'll just say it. I'm from a different universe."

"The fuck?" Trevor asked, while Misha simply exclaimed, "What?"

"Universe? Different *universe*?" Amavia asked.

"Like, triple hot!" Cheeky added. "Does that make you an alien? I've always wanted to…uh…*meet* an alien."

"You've heard of the multiverse theory?" Amanda asked. "Well, what can I say? It's true. There are other universes out there. Possibly an infinite number. Some are probably almost identical to this one, and others will be so alien, they might be incomprehensible.

"I know that you're probably thinking that this is crazy talk and impossible—something I would have said not all that long ago. But it was proven to me when an entity that lives between universes pulled me, Tanis, and several other individuals out of our worlds and into a construct that looked something like a saloon. We were unhurt, but coerced into telling stories, which is why Tanis talked about her and Cheeky meeting Maverick on the PetSil Mining platform." She glanced at Cheeky, who winked at her.

Nearby, Iris made a sucking noise, which got her a frown from Cheeky.

Amavia shrugged. "The multiverse is a widely accepted theory for us. Though I'd always wondered why we don't get more crossover."

"Well, I'm glad to help settle the debate," Amanda replied.

Jessica nodded, her expression not argumentative, but also not completely accepting. "So, why here, now?"

"I'll get to that. At the bar, Tanis and I got on well," Amanda said, "and when I was returned to my own universe, I resolved to find a way to visit. And, well, long story short… I did."

"How did you do that?" Iris asked.

"Okay, I knew this was coming, so, here goes. I came here by using Magic."

"I knew it," Cheeky exclaimed. "That's how you can use the Link!"

"I'm all for the multiverse, but magic's not real," Amavia commented flatly.

"As in hoodoo voodoo?" Iris asked, wiggling her fingers.

"Are you sure?" Jessica added.

"I believe it," Usef said. "I've seen some bizarre shit in my time."

"Me too," Misha agreed.

"Interesting," Jinx commented to Amanda. "Care to explain?"

"Sure," Amanda replied. "Okay, when I say Magic, that's just a word that people like me use to describe the powers that we can use. So, in my universe, some people are born with an ability to control an energy that we call Essentia. Essentia seems to be an extra universal force that seeps into other universes, such as mine and yours, and through our connection to it, we're able to make things happen."

"Like, what things?" Jessica asked, her tone curious.

~Well, I can speak directly into your minds with telepathy,~ she answered, sending her thoughts to everyone in the room. "I can also manipulate things like light and electricity," she said, and raised her hand.

As she did, a stream of light floated down from one of the fixtures above her and encircled her hand, dancing around her fingers, sparkling and glittering as it moved. She canceled the effect, and the light faded from view.

"I can move things, as well," she said.

Concentrating, she pulled on the Essentia around her once more. There was a whip-snap of air, and suddenly, Usef and Misha swapped places, each disappearing from one end of the table, and appearing at the other.

"What the hell?!" Usef hollered, half rising from his chair.

"Oh god, I feel sick," Misha groaned. "Give a guy a warning."

"Do me!" Cheeky said, then laughed. "I mean *move* me. Stars, I mean both, but not here for the other one."

"OK, that was impressive…" Amavia said as she leant forward. "It's almost as though you're ascended. Stars, I wish Finaeus were here to see this."

Jessica was frowning and glowing rather brightly as she regarded Amanda. "So, why are you here, and what do you need our help for?" she asked bluntly.

"Because I'm not the only Magus in your universe. There are others who have the ability to jump between worlds, and at least one of them is here on this station.

"I don't know how many there are, or what kind of team he or she might have with them, but they'll be here to steal or trade something…or recruit to their group. Maybe all three. I don't know, our intel on their mission is very limited. But what I do know is that I'm not familiar with this universe or this station, but you are, and I would dearly love for you to help, if you can.

"Will you help me?"

MULTIVERSAL

STELLAR DATE: 05.10.8948 (Adjusted Years)

LOCATION: *Sabrina*, Cerka Station

REGION: Mullens, Virginis System, LoS Space

Jessica's eyes widened, and she drew a deep breath, all too aware that everyone in the galley was staring at her.

"What? Just because I'm the general, *I* have to make the call on hunting interuniversal—I think I just made a new word—criminals?"

"Well, you're *also* the captain," Cheeky replied.

"Plus, Tanis told you to help Amanda," Iris added.

"Yeah, yeah." Jessica held up a hand to forestall any further admonitions from her crew. "Of *course* we're going to help stop these...magic users...from pilfering—" She paused and turned to Amanda. "What are they pilfering?"

The redheaded woman lifted her hands and shrugged. "Beats the hell out of me. What do you have around here that's worth stealing?"

Jessica glanced at Sabrina. "Well, the most valuable tech in a thousand light years are all on this ship."

"The station's been a bit unruly, but I haven't flagged any risks to the ship," the red and gold AI replied. "You'd think that if magic users were targeting me, and the rest of you, they'd, you know...."

"Actually target us?" Misha asked.

Usef glanced at the cook. "Or they're probing. Trying to see what avenues of attack are open to them. We need to understand these magic users' capa—"

"OK, wait." Cheeky held up a hand and smiled at Amanda. "You really don't go by 'magic users', do you? So what is it, are you a sorceress? A wizard? A magician? Are we up against warlocks?"

Amanda began to reply, but Jessica spoke up first. "And can they just teleport onto the ship like that? How do we defend against them?"

"Assuming their target is on the ship," Iris added.

All eyes turned to Amanda, and she met Cheeky's inquiring gaze. "Okay, one thing at a time. We call ourselves Magi, or Magus if there's only one."

"Magus...ooooh. Sounds so mysterious," Cheeky gave Amanda a saucy wink, and Jessica leant forward and gave her a light cuff on the back of her head.

"Focus, Cheeky."

Amanda laughed at the byplay and continued. "Also, sure, you might have some super tech on here, but that might not be what the Reavers are after. They might be here to recruit someone or trade with someone. We don't know their goal, which might have nothing to do with you guys. All I know is that we sensed a multiverse breach here, it's the Reavers, and we need to find out why.

"Reavers?" Trevor asked, an eyebrow cocked as he glanced at Jessica. "Sounds diabolical."

"A bit, yeah," Amanda replied. "Also, because this universe doesn't seem to have Magi, I would suspect that the Reavers will not be too blatant with their Magic. That would attract attention from people like me, and just attention in general. I think they'll use mundane methods as much as possible and be circumspect in their actions.

"Also, they probably don't know I'm here yet, so I need to keep a low profile for as long as possible. That means no excessive Magic use for the time being, because if there's a Magus close to me, they'll sense my pull on the Essentia."

Jessica ran a hand through her hair, forcing herself not to tug at it in frustration.

"OK," she said after a moment's consideration. "From what I gather, the Reavers likely came here because they used some sort of magic to detect something, or someone, that they desire. But if they're still hunting for it, they might not know exactly what or where it is yet, so they're hunting around for stuff that looks good."

"Best keep the stasis shields offline," Iris said, glancing at Sabrina. "My money says that it's either those, or the CriEn."

"What are those?" Amanda asked.

Jessica glanced at Iris, who shrugged before saying, "I mean…she's an extrauniversal magic cop who's friends with Tanis. If we can't trust her, who can we trust?"

Amavia laughed. "This might be my favorite conversation of all time."

"OK." Jessica turned back to Amanda. "Stop me if you have any of this stuff in your universe. CriEns are the easiest…sort of. Basically, there's a base-energy level to the universe. It's a part of the dark energy and the quantum foam that makes up everything. There's also a lot more of it than the observable energy in the universe. Sometimes it's called vacuum energy because it's present in a total vacuum. Either way, our ship has three of them, and they can draw *a lot* of power if we need it."

"How much?" Amanda asked.

"Enough to tear a hole in the very fabric of spacetime,"

Sabrina answered. "Or about as much as a star puts out in a second or two."

Amanda whistled, her eyes widening. "OK…I can see how that would be high on the Reavers' wish list."

"They're on everyone's list," Trevor said with a sardonic laugh. "A bit of a blessing and a curse."

"And stasis shields?" Amanda asked.

"Do you have any sort of stasis in your universe?" Jessica pursed her lips, wondering how to explain it. "Oh! Like cryostasis pods that people get put in if they have a long spaceflight ahead."

Amanda nodded quickly. "Yeah, of course, like the Marines on the *Sulaco* in Aliens, or Solo when he got frozen in carbonite!"

"Uhh…what?" Cheeky cocked her head. "What 'aliens'?"

"It's an ancient movie," Amavia explained. "I saw it once back on the Cho. And the other one is easy. That's from the old Star Wars vids."

Trevor snorted. "Which one? There are thousands of those."

"The originals," Amavia replied. "Stars…am I the only one here who knows any history?"

"This is so weird," Amanda said, shaking her head in

wonder. "All that stuff is from just a few decades ago for me."

"Well, some of us are from the forty-second century, and others are from the ninetieth, so we get the dissonance. OK, anyway," Jessica soldiered on, despite the curious look on Amanda's face. "Most people still use cryostasis for long spaceflight, but we have something that is true stasis, the total cessation of all atomic motion. It doesn't break the law of conservation of energy, and when used for ship's shields—something we have that no one else does—it creates an impenetrable barrier."

"Oh?" Amanda asked. "How impenetrable?"

"I smashed the ship into a planet once," Sabrina said, a smile quirking her lips. "Let's just say that I won, and the planet lost."

"Holy shit," Amanda whispered. "This ship is like a mini death star."

"A what?" Cheeky asked. "Is that a Magus thing? Or…Magi? Which is plural again?"

"OK, even I know that one." Trevor gave Cheeky a judging look. "It's from Star Wars again."

"It's such a classic." Amanda nodded vigorously. "You really should watch it."

"Getting back on track." Jessica glanced around the room.

"We also have better nanotech than most people, and—"

<*Keep our picotech a secret for now,*> Iris said privately.

<*Was planning on it.*>

The AI sent a mental affirmation. <*Right, but people know we're from the* Intrepid, *so they might assume we have picotech.*>

<*Right,*> Jessica said to Iris, then continued aloud, "and we have a line on an entire fleet of ships as powerful as this one."

"OK." Amanda blew out a long breath. "Sounds like a lot of that would be interesting to Reavers, especially if they could sell it to Riven…or use it to control them…."

"Riven?" Sabrina asked.

"Sorry." Amanda ducked her head. "People like you. Non-Magi."

Usef leant forward and placed his elbows on the table. "So then, can all Magi do what you just did? And can you teleport yourselves, too?"

Amanda nodded. "It's a learnt skill, like anything. As you get better, you can Port bigger things further, but we can assume that anyone who can get here can Port onto your ship. We can shoot lightning, see through things, scry other areas—"

"Wait, whosawhat?" Cheeky asked. "Scry?"

"Look at things from a distance. So, I can see what's

happening back in that police station while I'm sitting right here."

"Awesome," Cheeky replied. "Why not check out my room later on tonight," she suggested with a wink.

Amavia shrugged. "So other than teleporting, you're like a heavily modded person with a ship-level sensor suite that's undetectable. Shit…glad we don't have more people like you around."

Amanda gave a thin smile. "We are something of a nightmare for non-Magi."

"Well, there are ascended AIs," Jessica said, then lifted her hand, electricity arcing between her fingers. "Plus, shooting lightning isn't too hard."

"Is that from the alien microbes you mentioned back in the cell?" Amanda asked.

"Uh huh." Jessica nodded. "Though anyone could do it with the right mods. My power is just bio, not from an SC batt."

"Essy bat?" The redhead frowned.

Cheeky giggled. "Superconductor batteries. You can load them up with an incredible charge. We use them to power pretty much everything. Most—actually, all—of us have them in our bodies."

"Oh, that's what those are," Amanda replied, glancing at Cheeky's torso where Jessica assumed her SC batt was. "You're especially strange, Cheeky…I can't tell if you're human or an AI…." Amanda glanced up at Amavia. "Or you, either. You're like…two people, though."

"Lotta long stories," Jessica said. "Short version. Cheeky used to be a human, now she's an AI, and Amavia *is* two people."

"Huh." Amanda sat back in her seat. "And I thought most of the people I hang out with are weird. You're all cyborgs…."

"Cywhats?" Cheeky asked.

"People that are part machine," Amanda explained.

"You're the rare one," Jessica laughed. "A legitimate vanilla."

Amanda snorted. "I'm far from vanilla."

"Oh, I wondered about that," Cheeky said with a laugh.

"Are you leading me on, Cheeky? Because you might need to deliver on these promises," Amanda challenged her.

"Cheeky never leads people on. She always makes good on her innuendo," Jessica said, reaching out and patting the pilot on the head. "She does need to settle down, though. We need to decide what to do."

"I'm already sifting through the station's activity logs,"

Amavia said. "Looking for anything that stands out."

"Me too," Iris added. "But you saw the station tonight, Jess. Place is a mess."

"We might have to get out there and get our ears to the ground," she replied, heaving a long sigh.

"Do you really think it's wise for you to go out right now?" Usef asked. "The ship could be a target."

"Don't worry," Amanda said as she rose. "I'll put an Aegis on it. Not a heavy one—Magi on the station could detect that—but something that will alert me if anyone tries to Port aboard. Then I can bring us all back."

"What, all at once?" Iris asked.

"Uh huh," Amanda nodded.

"Jessica!" Cheeky turned, a cheek-splitting grin on her face. "Can we keep her?"

Jessica shrugged. "I don't see why not. We're living in the twilight zone…."

"Hey, that was a great show," Amanda replied.

"What's a show?" Jessica asked.

*****

After some brief preparations, the women were ready to

head back onto the station.

Jinx remained behind, unwilling to risk compromising a mission when she barely understood how to behave in public to begin with, which left Iris, Cheeky, and Jessica to accompany Amanda on the hunt.

"Is Jinx not coming?" Amanda asked.

"She's kinda new to being around people," Iris answered. "Until recently, she was imprisoned within a ship's navigation system and had no real exposure to the outside world. I think she'd rather not jeopardize the mission just to satisfy her curiosity."

Amanda nodded. "Understood. Shame, I liked her enthusiasm."

"So, are you going out dressed like that?" Cheeky asked.

Amanda eyed Jessica's and Iris's dresses, and then Cheeky's bikini.

"Good point, let's see," she said, and as Jessica watched, Amanda's shipsuit dissolved and was replaced by a slinky, metallic rose-gold mini dress.

"She's my date!" Cheeky called out and stepped up beside Amanda, threading her arm through hers.

Amanda didn't resist, accepting Cheeky's closeness with a smile.

"Looks about right," Iris said with a nod.

"Isn't that unusual?" Amanda raised an eyebrow. "Changing my clothes like that?"

"Not really," Jessica said with a shrug. "We can do stuff like that, too. Though I like buying clothing that never change into anything else—that sort of makes it feel more real."

"So, where's our first stop?" Iris asked as the four women walked out of the airlock.

"Well..." Jessica began as they walked out onto the concourse. "Amanda 'Ported' in only four decks down from where we encountered our group of crooks. Even with things being a bit of a mess on Cerka right now, two break-ins that close together is surprising."

"Surprising that they're close physically, or close time-wise?" Cheeky asked.

"Both," Iris replied. "They're not far from that ring's docks.... Let's go take gander and see what we can see. It's on the way to that Club Smash and Grab we were going to before, anyway."

"A 'gander'?" Cheeky giggled as the four women turned to the right and began strolling down the concourse.

"She likes to poke fun at my vocabulary," Iris said in an aside to Amanda.

Cheeky rolled her eyes. "And you like to find old words no one uses just to make people have to look them up."

"To be sure, at least she's not a pure haunty geebag and is goin' on the lash with us, cos that would be feckin' banjaxed lassy," Amanda replied, her Irish accent deepening as she spoke.

Jessica looked over at Amanda's utterance and saw the others giving her odd looks as well, only for Amanda to burst out laughing.

"Nothing like a bit of Irish slang to confuse people," Amanda explained.

"I understood it just fine," Iris replied with a shrug.

As Cheeky and Amanda joked about strange words and sayings, Iris reached out to Jessica.

<*So…do you really buy this? That it's all magic?*>

Jessica considered her response for a moment. <*Well…from what Finaeus told us, ascended AIs are rather amazing, and—if we were to use it wholesale—our picotech almost gives us matter transmutation abilities. Other than teleporting and this 'scrying', Amanda's magic really isn't that magical.*>

<*Right,*> Iris sent along a mental snort. <*Other than those two seemingly impossible things.*>

<*Well…there's a lot we don't know about the universe,*> Jessica

countered. <*What really intrigues me is how Amanda is clearly not ascended. From what both Finaeus and the records at Star City tell us, ascended beings can be—at least to us—non-corporeal. But other than her ability to teleport, Amanda is flesh and blood, just like us.*>

<*I wonder if…*> Iris began, then paused for a few seconds. <*If people from her universe have a genetic trait that has allowed for a branch of evolution that gives them a biologically inherited ascendancy. We should ask her for a DNA sample.*>

Jessica chuckled aloud, garnering the attention of both Cheeky and Amanda. "Sorry, just Iris. She wants a sample of your DNA, Amanda."

"Jess!" Iris exclaimed. "I was just musing! I don't really *want*-want it." She cocked her head to meet Amanda's eyes. "Unless you're offering."

"Ummm…Sure, if you'd like?" Amanda's reply carried a note of curiosity mixed in with uncertainty. "Trust me. People where I come from have spent a lot of time trying to find what makes Magi…well, Magi. Also, do you really want to let that cat out of the bag in your universe? From what I see on your networks, you have enough to worry about."

"Good point," Jessica eyed Iris. "Do you really want to have to deal with Magi teleporting in and out of places?"

Iris shook her head. "Okay, okay, I hear you. Let's keep

that genie in the bottle for now."

"The whosawhat?" Cheeky asked. "See, Iris, there you go again."

"You don't know what a genie is?" Amanda shook her head, laughing softly.

"Of course she does," Jessica said as they boarded a maglev. "Cheeky's the queen of messing with people."

"Why, Jessica!" Cheeky exclaimed. "You cut me to the quick!"

"See?"

The women settled into their seats, and the maglev train took off, whisking them away to their destination on the central spire, where they'd transfer to another line.

Jessica watched through the window as the car raced along the top of one of the ring spokes. Like the others, the spoke was covered with a transparent dome, and the majesty of Cerka's forty-kilometer length spread out around them.

She looked down at one of the freight docking rings, where a ship was being eased by tugs toward its grapple point, while ballast weights elsewhere on the ring shifted in anticipation of the new load.

The freighter was almost latched on when plasma and debris exploded from a nearby part of the ring. A section of hull plating flew out and collided with one of the tugs. The heavy lifter slewed to starboard, and its engines slashed across part of the ring, and then it broke free from the freighter.

With the shift in balance, the five-hundred-meter ship spun to port and slammed into the ring, crumpling a hundred meters of the station.

"Oh fuck," Jessica whispered, as she saw the reverberations ripple through the ring and along the spokes.

"The mounts on the spindle should compensate…" Iris said, leaning over Jessica to watch. "Sorry, was tapping your optics again. I like to look out through your eyes."

"I'm resigned to it," Jessica mumbled as emergency systems began to kick in, ballast shifting and the ring's retro jets firing to slow its spin.

The freighter fired its own maneuvering thrusters, pushing away from the station, the lone tug attached to its bow helping to right the ship as it eased out to a safe distance.

Left behind was a half kilometer of ring that was torn up and venting atmosphere.

"Shit…" Cheeky muttered. "It must have damaged the a-grav shields. That ring's bleeding air like there's no tomorrow."

"Seems a bit suspicious," Amanda said, her eyes meeting

Jessica's. "Perhaps we should investigate."

"Agreed," Jessica replied, sending a request to the maglev's NSAI controller to bring them down to the freight ring's nearest spoke.

REAVER ATTACK

STELLAR DATE: 05.11.8948 (Adjusted Years)

LOCATION: Cerka Station

REGION: Mullens, Virginis System, LoS Space

"The Maglev is diverting," Jessica informed the rest of the group.

Amanda glanced back down at the ring and the damage the ship had caused to it after the explosion. They needed to get down there fast. If the Reavers were still nearby, they wouldn't be for much longer.

She needed to see what was going on, and used her Magic to get a closer look. Her Magical vision scrying the area from just outside the lower ring, looking in through the hole caused by the explosion.

There were people inside, shooting at each other in what looked like a warehouse, judging from the crates.

"There's no time," Amanda replied to Jessica.

Quickly, Amanda picked a spot and reached out with her Magic once more, enveloping her new friends in Essentia. Light flashed behind her eyes, and a fleeting feeling of disorientation rushed through her as they Ported down to the ring below, appearing where Amanda wanted them to.

It was as if they had been dropped into the middle of a hurricane.

Wind whipped past them, catching their hair and dresses, as they all crouched to hide their presence. Smaller boxes and other detritus flew through the air as they were sucked toward the hole in the bulkhead and the void outside.

The girls had appeared out of immediate sight of the fighting nearby. They pressed themselves up against the nearest crates in an effort to get out of the wind.

"Shit," Jessica cursed.

<*Curious,*> Iris added, looking around. <*Station's a-grav fields are coming back online, though, they should have the hole in the hull airtight in a minute.*>

Amanda glanced at Cheeky, who was looking at her hands and then around her before a big grin spread over her face.

"That was *awesome,*" the blonde woman whooped, her exclamation drowned out by the wind and sounds of beam and gunfire from nearby.

Amanda didn't focus too much on her companions' reactions to being Ported, as a sudden feeling of exhaustion washed over her, hitting her hard. Already crouched down beside the container between Jessica and Cheeky, she felt her legs wobble, and she grabbed the crate to steady herself. The feeling passed, but for a few seconds, she'd felt surprisingly weak.

What the hell? What was that?

She was used to the disorientation from Porting, having used such Magic for over a thousand years now, but this was new. Though she felt short of breath from the thin air, she could tell that it wasn't the cause of her weakness. As her strength returned over the next few seconds, she wondered if there was something different about using Magic in this universe.

Something to be aware of, she thought.

<*Can you give us a warning next time? This place might have been in full vacuum…which we can handle, but it's a pain in the ass,*> Jessica scolded as the wind began to die down.

Amanda gave a silent nod, and Jessica's expression grew concerned.

<*Are you OK?*>

~I'm fine, just some dizziness. Multiversal stuff, probably,~ Amanda answered, already feeling back to her usual self.

<*Good. We can't have you crapping out on us now. We might need to beat a hasty retreat.*>

~I'm good, don't worry.~

Jessica nodded. <*Alright, we've got a nanocloud up. There are CPS teams over that way, and some well-armed thugs over here. Can you see if they're Reavers or not?*>

~Hang on,~ Amanda said, and with a thought, shifted her second set of senses, which were still active and outside the ring.

She brought them in and focused on the people that the cops were fighting. With her Aetheric Sight, she could see that the enemies were vanilla humans, but many of their weapons and armor was glowing with Essentia, marking them as enchanted.

~They're Reavers, but I can't see a Magus amongst them.~

<*You can see other Magi? They stand out?*> Jessica asked.

~Yep. Through my Aetheric Sight, anything Magical glows, including the bodies of Magi.~

<*Good to know. Hey, the a-grav shielding is running on just one emitter, and it's leaking. We need to clear these baddies out so the repair drones can get over there,*> Iris said while advancing to a new position that gave her a line of sight on the enemies.

Amanda focused her secondary senses on the damaged hull plating.

~I can fix that,~ she said, and concentrated.

Essentia surged, and as she conjured matter to fill the hole, she could feel the Magic draining her energy.

Curious, Amanda thought. It was also annoying, but not life threatening—at least, not directly. She'd think about it later, and for now, try to keep her use of Magic to simpler stuff.

Cheeky was staring open-mouthed at the now-sealed hole in the hull. <*Now, you don't see that every day.*>

<*Well, unless it's picotech,*> Jessica replied.

<*I've only ever seen that shred things apart,*> she countered. <*Plus, magic is way cooler than picotech.*>

<*Fascinating,*> Iris added.

With the hole filled, the howl of the environmental systems trying to keep the room pressurized diminished, and the sounds of weapons fire increased in volume as the air thickened around them.

Looking through her secondary senses, Amanda saw beams lance into crates and walls, while rail pellets cut through targets like butter. Nearby, a CPS agent was pulling an injured man back to safety, only to get his leg shot off by a kinetic round.

<*Alright, ladies, let's do this,*> Jessica said over the Link, sending a slew of data through a new channel.

The new Link channel was labeled as a 'combat net,' and

contained multiple views of the hold, lists of enemies, firing positions, and avenues of approach.

Amanda took a moment to review the data, and then assigned one of her other minds to the task as she looked up at the girls. She paused for a second upon seeing that they had begun stripping out of their clothing—well, Cheeky had already finished.

"What the hell?" she said, wondering what they were doing, when Iris suddenly disappeared.

<*Our stealth system is built into our skin. It can't cover our clothing,*> Jessica explained.

"Oh," Amanda said as a naked Jessica smiled at her before vanishing from sight.

Amanda turned to Cheeky, who was looking back at her with a coy smile as she twirled her bikini bottoms on a finger.

<*This was not how I thought you'd see me naked, but hey, treat it as a teaser.*> Throwing the tiny bit of fabric at Amanda, Cheeky winked and promptly disappeared.

"And you guys think *I'm* weird," Amanda commented as she caught Cheeky's bikini bottoms and pumped Essentia into her Aegis, topping it off. A separate working of Magic transformed her skimpy dress back into her bodysuit and boots, ready for action.

Through her Aetheric Sight, Amanda could still see the three women, despite their stealth. Her magical sight picked up their life signs and more as they began to make their way through the crates, moving to good firing positions.

A thought suddenly occurred to her, and with another quick working of Magic, Amanda conjured an Aegis around each of them. These invisible shields weren't super strong, but they'd mitigate the effect of any direct Magic sent their way in the short term.

Better safe than sorry, she thought.

A separate working of Magic by one of her multitasking minds bent light around herself, turning her invisible, but without removing her clothes as she crept forward with them. As the trio made for the main group, Amanda sensed life forms nearby.

~I'm hanging a left, got a couple of Reavers flanking us,~ she advised her companions.

<Need any help?> Jessica asked. *<I know Cheeky's keen to lend a hand.>*

~Bleedin' hell, the innuendos just don't stop around here, do they?~ Amanda exclaimed, her tone full of mirth.

<You better believe it,> Cheeky answered. *<I can think of at least two things I want to get my hands on.>*

Amanda laughed. *~The twins will be ready and waiting for you later, Cheeks. That's a promise. And don't worry, Jess, I'll handle these guys.~*

<We're never going to hear the end of this, are we?> Iris asked from her position, where she was already firing on the main group of Reavers.

<You mean the day Cheeky bedded a witch? No, probably not,> Jessica replied with a laugh.

<You're just jealous that she doesn't want you,> Cheeky said.

Jessica sent an image of her rolling her eyes through the Link. *<Alright, let's concentrate, ladies. We've still got…eleven of these idiots to deal with, and the CPS is way outgunned. I've told them to move back.>*

Pressing herself up against a crate, Amanda glanced back to watch Cheeky with her Aetheric Sight as the woman took aim with a pistol and fired on the Reavers.

Holy feck, she's hot.

Turning back to her quarry, Amanda waited as the four life forms approached her crate, thinking they were flanking her group. With Magic seeming to drain her, she had already decided to take these guys out the old-fashioned way.

A pair began to edge around the container she was hidden behind, their guns drawn and ready. They hadn't spotted her yet, though, her Magic hiding her from sight.

Waiting until just the right moment, Amanda lashed out and smashed the arm of the first man sideways into the crate. He dropped his gun with a clatter of metal and a yelp, his ulna and radial bones smashed.

Even as the first man groaned in pain, she brought her fist around and smashed it into the head of his partner, breaking the woman's jaw. Amanda then delivered a swift knee to her torso, making the Reaver woman gasp and drop to her knees with a gift of several broken ribs.

<*Wow, Amanda, you can really fight,*> Jessica commented approvingly over the combat net.

For a moment, Amanda was surprised Jessica had seen her moves, but then she remembered the omni-view of the room that the technology gave these women.

~*Was there ever any doubt? I've been alive a long time, and spent a lot of that training in martial arts,*~ she sent back, as she canceled her invisibility and brought her fist around in a hammer blow to the back of the first guy's neck. With a sickening crack, the man dropped limply to the floor.

<*Aaah, there you are,*> Cheeky said with a carefree laugh, followed by a sharp inhale. <*Oh crap. Dammit, these Reavers are good shots.*>

Without replying, Amanda turned and flipped over the gasping woman, simultaneously kicking the next two Reavers, knocking them back. She landed and spun, a boot lashing out again. It caught the guy on the left with a solid blow that sent him spinning head over heels before hitting the floor.

The fourth and final member of the flanking team stepped back and fired at Amanda, only to watch in alarm as the beam smashed into an invisible barrier in front of her target, and dissipated harmlessly. The Essentia in the gun delivered a little damage to her Aegis, but nothing she couldn't deal with.

She raised her hand and lightning flashed. The bolt slammed into the woman with a bang, and sent the Reaver flying back several meters. She smashed into a metal crate before dropping to the floor, leaving a bloody stain behind her.

Turning back to the other three enemies, Amanda saw the woman with broken ribs looking up at her, coughing as she attempted to raise her weapon in her quivering hand.

Amanda kicked the weapon out of the Reaver's hand, breaking a few metacarpals as she did so. With her Magic, she reached inside the Riven woman's unprotected head and made a tiny change. The woman slumped to the floor unconscious, like a rag doll.

A quick glance over the bodies around her confirmed they were all out of the fight, so Amanda moved back to where she could see the life signs of her friends.

She crept to a crate behind Jessica and the others, and looked around it to see the remaining Reavers rush forward, moving in concert and using their field of fire to keep Jessica and her team pinned down. Though it was mostly suppressive fire, it was well-managed, and Amanda could tell that they'd pinpointed the location of the invisible women.

Despite the onslaught, the women from *Sabrina* were undaunted, and moved to new positions, waiting for targets of opportunity before moving again, steadily wearing down the Reaver numbers.

Although none of the attacking Reavers were Magi, some of their weapons were glowing in Amanda's Aetheric Sight, marking them as enchanted. She also noted that some of them, notably the more accurate attackers, seemed to have Magically enhanced bodies as well.

Amanda frowned. With so much Magic around, she just had a feeling that there was bound to be a Magus close by, even if they weren't involved in the actual battle. She scanned the area, looking through her secondary senses as well, but nothing stood out.

As her gaze swept the scene, Essentia flared between her and the crew of *Sabrina*. With a snap of displaced air, a figure of a man appeared from nowhere, glowing brightly with Magical energy.

A Magus, finally.

Sudden, wickedly powerful electrical energy cracked through the air as a lightning bolt flew from the Magus and slammed into Jessica. Close to a hundred million volts flowed through the strike. Hotter than the surface of the sun, the bolt struck the purple woman, knocking her to the ground, where she spasmed for a moment.

Amanda stepped up to the enemy Magus and called on her own Magic. She summoned a kinetic ram of invisible force that hit him like a wrecking ball, sending him flying into a container before he hit the floor.

Looking over at Jessica, Amanda was pleased to see the woman up and moving. She gave a sigh of relief and turned her attention back to the Magus, who lay on his front, looking up at her with a knowing smile.

"I thought so," the Reaver said in a near whisper.

"Shite, no…" Amanda cursed, and moved to summon an Aegis around the room, pulling Essentia in as quickly as she could.

These moments of dizziness and weakness were really throwing her off her game and distracting her from some basic things she should be doing, like conjuring an Aegis around a fight like this.

With a whipcrack of air before she finished her work, the Magus Ported out. In the same instant, the remaining Reavers—the ones that were still alive—also disappeared.

"That is going to get *really* annoying," Jessica said as she approached, a look of worry in her eyes.

Amanda again felt far more out of breath than usual, and as her heart rate began to fall, the now-familiar feeling of weakness flushed through her. She crouched down and then fell to her ass, using her hands to steady herself and keep from collapsing completely.

"Are you okay?" Cheeky asked, rushing to Amanda's side.

Amanda gave a stoic smile and nodded as the feeling began to fade, her strength returning as quickly as it had left.

"I'm okay. Honestly. I think it's just a little harder for me to use my Magic here, or maybe I'm just not used to it—this whole, crossing into another universe thing. It seems to be taking a lot out of me."

Cheeky held out a hand, and Amanda took it, even though her legs were steady as she rose once more, her eyes on the group of Cerka police who were moving toward them.

TWO'S COMPANY

STELLAR DATE: 05.11.8948 (Adjusted Years)

LOCATION: Ring Nine cargo bay, Cerka Station

REGION: Mullens, Virginis System, LoS Space

"You keep busy, General," Detective Alla said by way of greeting.

Jessica looked up from the body she was standing over and nodded to the woman. "Sure seem to. Though I wish I wasn't. All I wanted was a night off, you know?"

"Night off?" Alla asked, laughing as she knelt next to the dead Reaver. "I don't even remember what those are, anymore."

"Me either." Jessica knelt as well. "I was trying to rekindle said memory, but no such luck."

The detective nodded absently as she pulled a pair of gloves on and began to look over the man. "Any idea who this guy is?"

"Part of a gang called the 'Reavers'," she said, deciding to give the detective at least that much information. "We think they're here to steal something, though we're not sure what."

Alla glanced up at Jessica. "Some of his gear is similar to those thugs you took out earlier."

"I noticed that too. Not sure if they're with this guy's group, or if they were just hired for a job."

The detective sat back on her heels, her eyes serious as she stared into Jessica's. "Well, this is a hell of a step up from a little break-in. Buggers wrecked a ship and blew a hole in the station! Not the sort of thing we can ignore."

"I know," Jessica replied. "General Hera is considering putting the entire station on lockdown, but with everyone finally just getting back to normal after the coup, she and the president are hesitant to make a drastic move like that."

Alla lifted her hands and rubbed both temples. "Looks like no sleep for me anytime soon, let alone a night off."

"We're scouring station security's cams," Jessica replied, rising from the dead Reaver. "We'll find where these bastards are operating from."

"Think so?" Alla asked as she also stood. "The CPS guys who were on-scene said that the bastards just disappeared. No trace on scan anywhere. With stealth tech like that, they could go anywhere on Cerka."

Jessica nodded, her thoughts turning to *Sabrina,* where she'd already ordered the crew to get armored and armed in case enemies appeared in their midst.

"Trust me," she replied after a moment. "I'm all too aware of that. Makes my skin crawl just thinking about it."

Alla stared down at the dead Reaver for a long moment and then sighed "Well, I guess we'd best get these bodies to the crime lab. We'll want to check them over and find out how their stealth works so well."

"Sorry, Detective," Jessica shook her head. "We're going to have to take possession of the bodies. I think my team is better suited to the task."

The woman standing on the other side of the body cocked her hip and her eyes narrowed. "Fine. I assume you have the admiral's backing on this?"

"I do," Jessica replied equably. "I'm not trying to step on toes, but given what we're dealing with here, we both know my team can learn a lot more about these Reavers and their abilities than your crime lab."

Alla's expression shifted from resentment to resignation. "Do you need me to arrange transport?"

"No," Jessica turned and nodded to a nearby airlock. Just beyond the viewports set into the hatch, the *Sexy—Sabrina*'s small pinnace—eased into view. "We'll transport them, though we won't object to a little help loading them up."

"Any chance I can send one of my crime analysts along to watch your people work?" the detective asked.

The question elicited a laugh from Jessica. "You're persistent, I like it."

With a wink and a rueful laugh, the detective turned and walked toward a group of CPS officers. Jessica watched her retreating for a moment, wishing that she could let the woman in on the truth, but it was just too much for someone to swallow and remain objective.

Not only that, but she had no idea if Alla might let it slip and send the station back toward general chaos. The detective did seem to genuinely care about Cerka, which made it unlikely that she'd spill something about visitors from another universe, but for now it was better safe than sorry.

<*Cheeky,*> Jessica called out, looking for the pilot, and unsurprised to see her emerge from the midst of a group of dockworkers who had been on the periphery of the scene.

<*What's up, Captain?*>

<*I want you to return to* Sabrina *on the* Sexy,> Jessica gestured to the pinnace, which was easing through the a-grav shield. <*I need you on the bridge, ready to rock, while the others go over the evidence.*>

Cheeky sent a mental snort over the Link. <*I assume that*

'others' doesn't include Misha?>

<Funny. No, it doesn't. I've told him to take scan on the bridge to keep him out of trouble.>

<What a way to spend a girls' night out—though I guess it's getting damn close to first shift, isn't it?>

<No rest for the weary, Cheeks. I suppose you can have Misha make a rousing breakfast for everyone at some point.>

The pilot laughed aloud as she walked across the dock, now angling toward where the *Sexy* was settling down between two rows of crates. *<This is* ***Misha****. I'd have to knock him out to keep him from retreating to his den to prepare a meal.>*

Jessica looked over the bay one more time, noting that none of the Reaver bodies had been disturbed, and then walked toward Iris and Amanda, both of whom were talking to a pair of the dockworkers who had been present when the Reavers had first attacked.

<Cheeky's going back with Amavia on the Sexy,> she advised Iris as she approached. *<How's our guest blending in?>*

<Better than you'd expect. Mostly, they're curious about her accent… It seems to have a special sort of effect on men. Quite fascinating, really.>

<It's Irish,> Jessica explained. *<Well, old-Irish, from my perspective.>*

Iris glanced at Jessica and rolled her eyes. *<Yeah, I know what it is. Between my own storage and* Sabrina's *databanks, I have access to all of ancient Terran history.>*

<You trying to make me feel old?>

<Is it working?>

Jessica didn't reply, instead listening in as the dockworkers explained that they'd been preparing for the inbound cargo ship when they spotted several of the Reavers opening shipping containers destined for Sarneeve.

"Any idea what was in the containers?" Amanda asked.

The two men looked at one another, and one shrugged before replying, "Not one hundred percent, no. Several of the containers were empty, on their way to be filled with supplies, and a few were military hardware, though I'm not sure what."

"They all got blown out into space, though," the other man said. "Tugs are going to have a field day trying to clean that mess up."

<I'm looking over the manifests,> Iris said on a private channel with Jessica and Amanda. *<Scanning what's left with our drones, and using process of—oh wow….>*

<Enough drama,> Jessica chided. *<What did you find?>*

<Looks like they were shipping out the remains of the proton cannon tanks we destroyed during the coup. Sending them off to a

decommission facility. A bunch of other hardware from the fight in there, too.>

<*Certainly suspicious,*> Jessica commented.

<*What is?*> Amanda asked.

<*During the recent attempt at a coup here, we went up against some pretty serious tanks. After the fight, we discovered that they, and a few of the combat mechs, were being operated by brain cases. Pretty sick stuff.*>

Amanda cocked an eyebrow. <*'Brain cases'? That sounds gross.*>

<*Very.*> Iris's tone was entirely dispassionate. <*They're literally brains…in cases. No human body, but forced to follow orders and be the perfect soldiers. Really inefficient, but some people get it in their heads that those are better than NSAI bots.*>

<*Wow…*> Amanda shook her head in disbelief. <*That's some sick shite.*>

<*Uh huh,*> Jessica agreed. <*There's a lot of coercion tech in play. Decent stuff, too. I could see someone with loose morals using it to have full control over their underlings, or to grow their army's ranks quickly.*>

<*Think that's the target?*> Iris asked while thanking the workers and dismissing them.

Jessica nodded. <*Worth following up on, at least.*>

"General Keller!" a voice called out to her left, and she turned to see Alla approaching.

"What is it, Detective?"

"I've just gotten word there have been a half-dozen break-ins across the station in the last hour."

"It's a big station," Iris said. "And you said that crime is up. That number doesn't seem too alarming."

The detective nodded. "Yeah, but this is in addition to the regular petty stuff. All of these break-ins were at military storage facilities."

Jessica glanced at Iris. "Well, shit. What got stolen?"

"That's just the thing. From what we can tell, nothing—except for at one depot that had components for those tanks the VDF uses."

"The ones with the proton cannons?" Jessica asked, glancing at the other two women.

"Yeah, nasty things. Still can't believe what they were operated by."

"Thanks, Detective. Pass me the data on those," Jessica said. "We're going to go take a look at the scenes."

* * * * *

Upon review of the break-ins, Iris spotted an inventory discrepancy at a military munitions depot, and separated to investigate that, calling on Jinx to aid her in the investigation, while Jessica and Amanda continued on to the facility where the proton tanks were stored.

"Are you sure you can't just teleport us there?" Jessica asked as the two women sat in an unoccupied maglev car.

"Well…between you and I, I've been feeling a bit weak when I use my abilities here. I almost passed out after fighting off that other Magus. I think I'll be OK, though…so long as I don't go Porting groups of people around."

"OK, but after this, we should swing back around to *Sabrina* and get you a regular weapon," Jessica suggested. "Just in case you conk out again."

"That's not a bad idea. Better safe than sorry," Amanda answered.

"So, do you think it's likely that the Reavers are after the mind control tech so they can build up some sort of army?"

Amanda shrugged. "To be honest, I don't really know what they're planning to do with anything. But I'll admit that *someone* might want the ability to make a machine-zombie army."

Jessica snorted at the idea, and then pursed her lips as she considered it further. "You know…I guess that's kinda accurate. And makes it so much worse."

"Happy to help."

They had to change maglev lines twice to get to where the break-in had occurred, finally arriving at a public warehousing district that the Virginis Defense Force had taken control of to store equipment and munitions.

As such, the security was almost an impromptu affair, utilizing human patrols and drones that roved the corridors around the warehouse blocks.

"Not sure about this being your Reavers," Jessica said as they passed under a half-destroyed security arch. "This thing was shot to shit on the way in, from the looks of it. Your friends could have just Ported in."

"Maybe," Amanda replied. "Or maybe my counterpart is feeling worn out like I am."

Checking the timestamps on the attack, Jessica saw that it had occurred just minutes after the Reavers had Ported out of the shipping bay on the lower ring. If they were facing just one enemy Magus, chances were that they would be too tired to do it again—but she wasn't prepared to assume they were only squaring off against a single enemy.

Once through the destroyed security arch, they met with

the commander on the scene, Major Olaf.

“It’s weird,” he said while leading the pair of women into the warehouse that had been hit. “It’s one half smooth op, and the other half smash and grab.”

“Oh?” Amanda asked as they strode past rows of containers and caged-off sections filled with weapons and munitions.

“Yeah.” The major nodded toward a cage that had been cut open. “Whoever did that was sloppy…and a little dumb. They probably spent a few minutes with a plasma cutter to get through the wire, when they could have just cut the lock open.”

“Does seem a little silly,” Jessica agreed. “So where are the smooth parts?”

“Over here.” The man stopped in front of a pair of opened containers that held a pair of proton tanks. “These two were accessed by someone who had the codes. Only thing is, they didn’t take anything. Only looked inside for a minute, from what we can tell.”

“Caught them on the feeds?” Jessica asked.

“Sort of, there was a lot of interference—some type of jamming tech—but the logs show when the doors were opened, and we got a clear view just three minutes later. But they were already gone."

"Doesn't seem like enough time to get anything..." Amanda said. "I don't think these proton tanks are what they're looking for."

"They?" the major asked.

"Just a hunch, Major," Jessica replied. "We're operating on the assumption that these break-ins are connected to the attack down on Ring Nine. From what we can see, they might have been after the proton tanks down there that were shipping to Sarneeve."

Amanda shook her head, turning to look around the warehouse. "Except that if that's what they were looking for, why did they leave without so much as touching them?"

"A really good question." Jessica drummed her fingers on her thigh as she walked into the first container, confirming that the access panel to where the brain case would normally be stored was untouched.

"We checked it," the major said. "These tanks had their control tech removed last week, though. They're slated to get refitted to use NSAIs."

"Just had to check," Jessica shrugged. "You know how it is."

"Sure."

"So from what I see, all that got stolen were small arms and ammunition from some of the cages."

"Yeah, petty stuff, in all honesty," the VDF officer replied.

"When did your forces arrive?" Amanda asked.

"I didn't get here till ten minutes before you. We lost our two guards, so station police were first on scene—our military police were running all over already."

Jessica met Amanda's gaze. *<A lot of chaos. Whoever this is, they are really orchestrating things well.>*

The red-haired woman nodded soberly. *<They are, and we're no closer to knowing what they're really after—though it still could be that mind control tech. The Magus could have checked those tanks over without tampering with them.>*

<Great,> Jessica shook her head as she thanked the Major for his time. *<So it could be that they're really after that, or any other thing on the station.>*

<Say hello to square one.>

As they walked out of the warehouse, Jessica spotted a small security drone laying on the ground behind a crate. It had been shot and smashed, but the scan-dome was intact.

"What's that?" Amanda asked as Jessica picked it up, feeding a nanofilament into the device.

"Well." Her brow lowered in concentration. "It's probably

nothing. Looks like the storage card is shot…literally. But there just might be something in the buffers…."

She connected her nanofilament directly to the optical sensors and fed power into them. They initialized and began their reset, but she quickly halted that process and checked the temporary storage.

"Bingo!"

"Found something?" Amanda asked.

Jessica set down the drone and held up her hand, displaying a holoimage of a man and a woman fleeing the warehouse.

"They look scared," Amanda commented as Jessica started the playback and it caught a full visual of the woman's face.

"Not as much as they're gonna be when we come to visit them," she replied.

"You have an ID?"

Jessica nodded. "That is Alma Ameris. She's the captain of a privateer ship that has a bit of a reputation for getting up to mischief."

"Well, that rules them out, then," the Magus said. "My guess is that they're running from the Reavers, not working with them."

"Sure," Jessica nodded as she led the way out of the

warehouse. "But that doesn't mean they didn't see anything."

A mischievous grin crept onto Amanda's lips. "Then, I assume you know where their ship is berthed?"

Jessica matched the other woman's expression. "Wouldn't you know that it's just a ten-minute walk from here. They've put in for a departure, but the STC—"

"STC?" Amanda interrupted.

"Space traffic control," Jessica explained. "Sorry, sometimes I just rattle off acronyms. Anyway, the STC has halted all departures until the mess down on Ring Nine gets cleaned up."

Amanda laughed. "Nice to have a silver lining."

"Let's go see what our friend Alma saw. Maybe we can turn a silver lining into a solid lead."

TAKING A TOLL

STELLAR DATE: 05.11.8948 (Adjusted Years)

LOCATION: En route to Alma's ship, Cerka Station

REGION: Mullens, Virginis System, LoS Space

"It's quiet here," Amanda commented as she walked along the concourse with Jessica.

They'd been walking for nearly ten minutes and had left the warehouse district behind. A few blocks on, Amanda figured they must be in one of the less savory areas of the station. There was more trash in the corridors, and the shops and units were sealed up or empty and looted. The ones that were open for business had protective grating over their windows, and holo-graffiti covering their walls.

Even the people seemed to have lost all hope.

"Bad neighborhood," Jessica replied. "It's not unusual in stations this big."

"I guess after the coup, it's going to take a while to clean everything up. What was it all about?"

"The liberation of AIs who've been used basically as slaves for too long, coupled with the AST's occupation of the outer

Virginis System. We kinda started it twenty years ago, when we came through here and Sabrina showed some of the AIs what it meant to be free. One thing led to another, and eventually, fighting broke out. We're here to help make that right."

"Sounds like you're cleaning up some of your own mess a little bit."

Jessica shrugged. "I guess you could put it that way. We're trying to make things better, but people can be resistant to change."

Amanda nodded. "Yeah, I know all about that."

"Oh?"

"Well, it's complicated, but back in my universe, I'm part of a small group who are joining a large, well established organization called the Nexus. Some of the member states of the Nexus don't like the idea of us becoming members. It means change, which they're resistant to. Also, I think they see it as a power grab, so they're fighting us. I can see it getting violent before long."

"The liberation of the AIs is having a similar effect," Jessica said.

"Hey, ladies, what you doin' down here, lookin' all shiny an' shit?"

Amanda looked up to see a man leaning against the wall, looking them over and licking his lips. He looked as though he could do with a good long bath and a new set of clothes.

"You don't wanna know," she replied as they walked past, and then glanced down at Jessica's fitted, shimmering purple bodysuit—which she had changed into after the Reaver attack—and her own glossy white one. "I guess we don't exactly blend in," she commented to Jessica as she glanced back at the man, who was watching them walk off.

"Well, no time to worry about that now, the berth is just ahead on the right."

Amanda followed Jessica's gaze and saw that the large loading doors were wide open. They moved closer, slowing down as they went.

~*Shall we have a peek inside?*~ Amanda asked, as she saw a cloud of nanoscopic machines sweep off of Jessica like smoke in her Aetheric Sight. They'd be invisible to the human eye, but she could see their energy signatures quite clearly.

<*Certainly,*> Jessica replied.

An image appeared through the Link. Beyond the door, Amanda could see a large bay with a few crates inside, and an airlock on the far wall, which was currently open. Between the two doors, a group of people stood talking.

As Amanda watched, she quickly realized it was actually two groups, and they seemed to be having something of a heated debate.

~What's going on here?~ Amanda asked as they stopped beside the door.

<I don't know,> Jessica replied.

Then the audio began filtering through the feed from Jessica's nano.

"Don't play coy with me, Alma," a man said. He stood at the fore of one of the groups and was addressing a woman wearing a defiant expression, surrounded by several men and women who were giving off some strong, 'don't fuck with us' vibes. "I know you got something from there. Was this another one of your little excursions, or are you working for someone?"

<Local help for the Reavers, maybe?> Jessica asked.

~Maybe,~ Amanda said, unsure. *~Sorry, I really wish I knew more.~*

<Don't fret it, we'll find them, one way or another.>

"Hey, shiny hiney, did no one tell you snooping was rude?" a voice yelled out from behind them.

They looked around just in time to see the dirty man who had catcalled them earlier striding down the passage toward them with his weapon raised. A moment later, he fired.

Amanda ducked and moved to the side. Jessica did the same, dashing into the loading bay. Amanda tucked herself behind a stack of crates as shouting broke out from the two groups of people they had been spying on.

She looked up to see that Jessica had gone the other way once through the door, and was nearly ten meters away, firing at the lookout with her gun. She hit him in the shoulder, burning his arm off and knocking him to the floor.

For the first time since her initial arrival, Amanda felt nervous. With her Magic use severely limited, the prospect of a fight actually gave her pause. She wouldn't normally run from a fight, but this was different. She was in another universe, dealing with highly advanced tech that she wasn't familiar with, and facing the possibility that she might pass out at any given moment from the strain of using her Magic.

She wasn't totally convinced that fighting these guys was a good idea.

~Stay or go?~ she asked over the Link, as the noise of gunfire filled the room.

A fight had broken out between Alma's pirates and the other group, and several shots slammed into the floor around Jessica and herself. Amanda looked toward the door. The man outside that Jessica had shot was pushing himself up with his one good arm, looking confused.

Concentrating as she waited for Jessica's response, Amanda flushed more Essentia into her Aegis, which she had left untouched since the Reaver attack. There was no avoiding using her Magic now, though. She needed its protection.

Still, she'd felt better this last hour or so....

Maybe I'll be alright?

<*Stay and take them on,*> Jessica advised. <*I want to know if any of these guys are involved in the Reavers' operation.*>

She nodded to Jessica as the one-armed man looked in Amanda's direction and fumbled with his gun. Amanda concentrated and hit him with a small but powerful kinetic punch to his temple, knocking the man unconscious. When she looked over at Jessica, she found that she'd already moved.

Get it together, Mandy, she thought to herself. *You might not be able to use your Magic as you'd like, but you can kick these guys' arses easily enough.*

She took a deep breath and focused her mind. She had a job to do. Void was relying on her; now was not the time to get nervous about a fight.

She ducked around the crates she was crouching beside to

see the gang who'd been talking to Alma's group taking cover ahead of her. The immediate impression she got was that these guys were no two-bit Mickey Mouse operation, but heavily armed, competent fighters.

"Shit," she hissed to herself, her nerves returning in the form of butterflies in her stomach. *I might need to use my Magic to do this,* she thought.

"Hey," one of the gang members shouted. He was close by, and swung his gun around to bring it to bear.

Amanda moved and ran for him, ducking right as he fired, and then she was suddenly right on him. Two shots slammed into her Aegis and ricocheted off her Magical shield before she swung out and slapped his gun to the side, and then backhanded him across the face with the same hand, moving with a superhuman speed.

Blood flew as he yelled in pain. She followed up with a punch to his gut, doubling him over, before she kneed him in the face.

A man next to her target, who had been trying to get shots in at the other group and not paying her much mind, suddenly turned and fired at her, the energy blast from his gun smashing into her Aegis. On instinct, she lashed out with a kinetic ram. The energy rushed out of her and hit the man, flinging him into the crates he was hiding behind.

Amanda felt another wave of dizziness wash over her.

Shite, maybe I'm not over it yet.

She staggered back and looked left to see one of the gang members pull a huge cannon from his back and aim it toward where she was fairly sure Jessica was, but she could only reach for a box to steady herself as the man fired.

There was a huge explosion on the other side of the room, and then the leader of the gang shouted at the man with the cannon and pointed.

Without hesitation, the shooter swung around and fired at her.

Amanda Ported. She hadn't moved far, but the direction had been random, another reaction based purely on instinct and without much of a plan.

There was more shouting, but her vision was swimming badly. She leant against the wall and looked up as another figure fired at her. Her Aegis flared as it protected her, but the stress of the Magic use was too much, and her vision began to tunnel.

The shooting at her stopped amidst more shouting, and then everything went dark.

DUKING IT OUT

STELLAR DATE: 05.11.8948 (Adjusted Years)

LOCATION: Cerka Station

REGION: Mullens, Virginis System, LoS Space

"Hey, shiny hiney, did no one tell you snooping was rude?"

Jessica's feed from her nanocloud showed the man they'd passed in the corridor approaching from the rear…with a railgun.

"Shit!" she swore as he fired, diving into the loading bay and rolling behind a stack of crates.

The shot streaked past and struck a bulkhead near where the two gangs stood. After a cursory check that Amanda had gotten to cover on the far side of the entrance, Jessica spun and let fire with her electron beam, burning off the attacker's right arm and relegating him to the 'no longer a threat' category.

Maybe wear armor next time, buddy.

She turned back to the two gangs, both of which were yelling at one another as weapons were drawn, and readied herself for a fight.

<Stay or go?> Amanda asked, and Jessica almost laughed.

She couldn't remember the last time she'd run from a fight. She was aware that Amanda had been suffering recently, though, and wondered if that was putting a dent in her confidence.

<Stay and take them on, I want to know if any of these guys are involved in the Reavers' operation.>

She saw Amanda nod, and turned her focus back to the gangs, who had been distracted from yelling at one another by her shooting the lookout.

Weapons fire rained down on her position, and Jessica flipped her flow armor from an iridescent purple to invisible. She moved to a new position and unslung her rifle, lobbing a few concussive crowd control shots into the largest cluster of gang members.

Out of the corner of her eye, she saw Amanda charge another group of them, their rounds ricocheting off an invisible shield that protected the Magus.

Shit…need to teach her to use a rifle for starssakes.

She was about to move to better cover her partner, when a wave of pulse blasts hit the stack of crates she was hiding behind, knocking the topmost one off. It hit her in the shoulder, but her flow armor solidified around the impact, distributing the force.

It was still unpleasant, and Jessica muttered a curse as she moved around the stack into a new position and fired her arm-mounted electron beam at the woman with the pulse canon.

She'd meant to hit the shooter's arm, but at the last minute, the woman dodged to the side, and the relativistic stream of electrons cut the thug in half.

"Shit," Jessica muttered. She'd wanted to be as non-lethal as possible with these enemies—as much to question them later as that she hated the idea of mowing down people with inferior armor and weapons.

Across the room, a stack of crates went flying, several slamming into gang members and sending them sliding across the deck.

<*Iris, where are you?*> Jessica called out.

<*I'm with Jinx, same ring as you, just two klicks downspin.*>

A few more shots came her way, and Jessica returned fire before responding. <*Get over to my location. We're having a fun dock fight.*>

<*What?*> Iris feigned an injured tone. <*And you didn't invite me?*>

<*Was a spur of the moment thing. Hurry.*>

<*We're already in a car.*>

Jessica fired a few more shots at the enemies near the ship's entrance, trying to advance so she could cover Amanda, as the Magus carved a path toward Alma, who was backing toward the ship.

She was about to tell the other woman to hold up when she caught sight of one of the thugs pulling a concussive RPG launcher off his back.

"Oh fuck!"

She broke cover, running almost straight for the shooter while praying her stealth would hide her well enough that he wouldn't see the blurred edges of her form as she raced across the deck.

A second later, the man fired, and the RPG streaked past Jessica, striking her former hiding place and blasting crates in all directions.

The members of both gangs moved in, firing wildly as they worked to keep her pinned down as they cleared the debris in search of her body.

Of course, Jessica wasn't there anymore.

She'd almost reached the man with the launcher, when he pivoted and fired at Amanda. A wordless scream tore from Jessica's throat as she slammed into the shooter, knocking him to the ground and sending the launcher flying. She tripped over his leg and fell, rolling to her feet a second later. She searched for Amanda, who was nowhere to be seen.

For a second, she thought the other woman had been completely vaporized, but remembered that teleporting was now a thing.

"Freeze!" a voice yelled from behind her, and Jessica turned to see Alma holding a railgun. "Your stealth's good, but you picked up some grime on the deck. Show yourself."

Jessica disabled her stealth, turning slowly and surveying the bay. The other gang was retreating to the station, while Alma's crew was moving back to their ship. She saw both sides carrying wounded, but the concussive blasts had dispersed her nanocloud, and she couldn't see if any were transporting Amanda.

"Shit," Jessica muttered, settling her flow armor to reveal her face. "What a day."

Alma's eyes widened as she realized who was standing on the other end of her rifle. "Oh, damn…you're General Keller."

"Yeah," Jessica replied as she dusted off her arms. "And you're Alma, right? Petty thief?"

"Ship captain," the other woman corrected, drawing herself up. "And I think I just pulled in a major haul."

It was clear that she intended to take Jessica hostage when

she nodded for two of her nearby crewmembers to approach her prize.

"If you touch me, I'll melt your skin off," Jessica warned the woman on her left. "I'm sure you know what I can do."

"Shoot lightning from your hands?" Alma asked. "Trickery. Now get on the ship. I bet we can get a million credits for you."

Jessica sighed and held her hand up for the gang leader to be silent.

<Iris, how close are you?>

<Five minutes.>

<One of the gangs here bailed. I think they might have Amanda, but I'm not sure.>

The AI sent an incredulous snort. *<How can you not be sure?>*

<She teleports, remember? I don't know where she went, or if it was of her own volition.>

<OK…that makes sense,> Iris replied. *<I've got visuals on that other gang leaving, though they're all wearing scan-cloaks to hide their idents. Not sure if our sorceress is with them.>*

<I'm leaving them to you, I'll see what my new friend Alma knows.>

Iris laughed. *<Be gentle.>*

<*Why would I do that?*

<*Good point. I'll update everyone else.*>

"I'm not sure you know how this works," Alma said while Jessica finished her conversation with Iris. "I've captured you, so now you have to do what I say."

"Yeah, sure," Jessica nodded as she turned and began walking toward the ship's open cargo airlock. "Let's go already. CPS is gonna be here any minute."

Alma and her two companions shared confused looks and then followed Jessica onto the ship, one stopping to close the airlock while the captain kept her rifle trained on their captive.

"Seriously, General, we're not just going to let you wander around our ship. You're going into our brig."

"Brig?" Jessica cocked an eyebrow. "This little tub has a brig?"

"It's a bigger ship than your *Sabrina,* and yes."

"Size doesn't count for everything. Trust me."

"This chick's weird," the man beside her said.

Jessica turned to the man as she felt the telltale vibration of the ship undocking. "I'll take that as a compliment."

He stepped closer, and Jessica reached out and grabbed him by the neck. His hands came up, ineffectually clawing at his wrist as she lifted him off the ground.

"Don't," Alma growled, pulling her railgun against her shoulder. "I don't want to have to kill the golden goose."

A burst of energy flowed from Jessica's hand into the man's neck, and he went unconscious.

"Yeah, let's not do that," she replied, opening her hand and letting the thug fall.

"Shit," whispered the woman who had mocked Jessica's ability to shoot lightning a minute before.

Alma's eyes had widened, but she still had her weapon trained on Jessica. "Brig. Now!"

"Captain," Jessica shook her head. "You don't seem to understand what's happening here. I'm not your captive. I came here to ask you what you saw in those containers when you broke into the VDF's storage facility. If your dumbass out on the dock hadn't shot at us, we'd just be having a friendly conversation right now."

"Really?" Alma's rifle lowered a centimeter. "We *did* break into a VDF facility," the woman reminded her.

"Well, *mostly* friendly, then. I'll still have to turn you over to the CPS after."

"Like fuck that's happening."

<*Sabrina, you coming?*> Jessica called out.

<*Oh…you mean you need help?*> the AI asked. <*I thought you*

were just going to lone-ranger yourself off that ship.>

<*We need to stop watching so many old vids.*>

The AI giggled. <*Hi-ho Silver, away!*>

<*Does that mean you're coming?*>

<*No, we're taking on bodies from another attack. I feel like a freakin' morgue. Trevor's on his way to the* Sexy, *though.*>

<*OK, Sabs.*> Jessica sighed, knowing Trevor would be annoyed with her. <*Hey, hon, you have a lock on the ship I'm in?*>

<*Don't 'hon' me,*> Trevor grunted. <*You know it's too dangerous to go solo out there.*>

<*I was with our friend the witch-queen, but she went poof. I'm trying to figure out if she's on this ship, plus interrogating its captain.*>

<*How's that going?*>

<*Poorly, they don't seem to understand who's captured who.*>

Trevor laughed. <*OK, well, they're pulling away from the station, and Cheeky's linked with the STC, asking them not to shoot while you're aboard.*>

<*How kind,*> Jessica chuckled aloud. <*Shoot, they're yelling at me now. I need to focus.*>

<*I'll be at the airlock in ten, ready to kick ass.*>

<*Looking forward to it.*>

"If you don't move your ass in the next three seconds, I'm

gonna—"

Alma's shriek cut off as Jessica reached out and placed her hand on the end of her railgun.

"You need to relax, Captain," she said, releasing a passel of nano onto the weapon. "Or shoot. Pick."

"What the hell is wrong with you?" Alma sputtered.

"It's like this," Jessica said, glancing at the other three crew members who had entered the cargo bay while she'd been speaking to Trevor. "You're not really a significant threat to me. I also want to get intel from you, so I'm not killing you. I need to find out if my friend is on your ship. Actually, let's start at the end there. Is my friend on your ship?"

"Your friend? The redhead?"

"Yeah, she's a witch. I think red hair is their calling card."

Alma cocked her head. "For real?"

"No, I have no idea if all witches have red hair."

"Fuck," the captain shook her head and yanked her railgun out of Jessica's grasp. "I think you're crazy. Boys, grab her and toss her in the hole before I get a worse headache."

Two of the crew advanced on Jessica, seizing her arms and pulling them back.

Splaying her hands, she reached out and grabbed onto the first things she met. One was a hip, and the other was a man's junk. A hundred thousand joules of energy flowed into each, and amidst a pair of blood curdling shrieks, the hands grasping her arms let go.

Around her, the rest of the ship's crew backed off, though Alma's jaw tightened.

The woman knew she had to show her crew that she was still in control of the situation, but Jessica was too valuable a prize to simply kill. With a look of forced resolve, she pursed her lips and lowered her railgun, aiming at Jessica's leg.

"You're gonna regret that," she informed her reluctant prisoner.

Her finger pressed the firing stud, but nothing happened.

"Oh shit," someone said.

Jessica strode forward, snatched the rifle from Alma, and grabbed the woman by the hair.

"OK, lady. I'm starting to get annoyed. You're going to tell me everything you know."

*****

Fifteen minutes later, Trevor walked onto the bridge, a laugh bursting from his throat as he saw Jessica lounging on the captain's chair, legs hanging over one arm while her head rested on the other.

"This your new ship?" he asked, looking around.

"Stars no!" Jessica snorted. "Did you catch a whiff of the smell in the passageway out there? What *makes* that sort of stench, anyway?"

Her husband shook his head. "I really don't want to know. Smelled like hydraulic grease and dead skunk."

"Guh…there's a terrible visual."

"So, where's the crew?" he asked, turning as Jessica nodded to his left.

All nine members of Alma's crew were lined up along the far side of the bridge, foreheads on the deck, hands cuffed behind their backs.

"Damn, that looks uncomfortable," Trevor muttered. "Reminds me of that one time we all went on a team-building event with Cheeky."

"Trevor! We all swore never to speak of that again."

"I didn't speak of, it, I spoke of being reminded of it."

"Same difference."

He shrugged. "Well, did you learn anything from them?"

Jessica swung her legs over the edge of the chair and stood, stretching languidly. "Damn, that was uncomfortable."

"Then why were you doing it?"

"To get a laugh out of you when you came in," she replied.

The mountain of a man shook his head, a deep rumble sounding in his chest. "I suppose it worked, then. You do love to make a scene."

"*Set* a scene, Trevor. 'Make a scene' sounds like I throw hissy fits or something."

"I know."

Jessica laughed and turned to the crew. "OK, so Amanda's not on board—hopefully Iris finds her soon. Once I determined that, I got them to tell me what they saw in the weapons depot. Was definitely our evil warlock guy—"

"Magus, Jess, he's called a Magus."

"Sure," she nodded. "But how often do we call people what they want?"

"Ummm…pretty much most of the time."

"Spoilsport." She shot her husband a mock glare before continuing, "I guess he was doing some sort of hoodoo voodoo on the proton tank. Probing it with magic—which scared them off."

"That probably explains why you didn't see any tampering on the tanks."

"Right," Jessica nodded. "Also confirms that they're here looking for the mind-control tech that the VDF was using on their brain cases."

"So is there any of that left?" he asked. "Other than in the crates that went boom down on the lower ring."

"Not that I know of," she replied. "But I want to go visit General Hera just to be sure."

"Once we deal with this," Trevor said, then held up a hand. "No, don't you dare take the *Sexy* and leave me with this lot. No, no, no."

"Pleeeaase, the smell is killing me."

"Fine." He kissed her forehead. "But you owe me. Big time."

Jessica gave him a winning smile. "Anything."

"You're going to play the next four games of snark with a four-card handicap."

"Shit," she muttered. "You drive a hard bargain."

*****

<Jinx, you ready for this?> Iris asked. *<We kick ass, take names, and get Amanda out.>*

The other AI checked her multimode railgun and the electron beam on her right arm. *<I'm more than ready. But we have to keep them alive?>*

<Well, the majority of them. Don't take any damage just to keep one of them alive, though.>

<OK, I can work with that. Think Amanda is in this place?>

Iris stared down the long corridor that led into an old waste reclamation plant.

<I mean…I hope so. If Amanda's not in there, she's lost. But at the same time, I kinda hope she teleported to a spa and has been too busy getting her feet rubbed to message us.>

<Is that a thing? Getting your feet rubbed?> Jinx asked.

Iris laughed aloud. *<Stars…with how often Jessica asks Trevor to do it for her, you'd think it was the* ***only*** *thing.>*

The pair of AIs began to advance down the corridor, a nanocloud flushed out ahead of them, searching for any sensors—not that they'd be likely to pick up the two stealthed figures.

<So what do you think of all this magic stuff?> Jinx asked as they approached the sealed doors at the end of the passage. *<Is it for real?>*

<It has to be,> Iris replied. *<Because she freakin' teleported us from a maglev car to the docks. And the timestamps on the local networks confirmed that it was instantaneous.>*

<What is that, then? Some sort of matter-quantum-tunneling effect?>

<*Honestly?*> Iris asked as she reached the door and placed a breach kit on the panel. <*I'd rather just think of it as magic. Makes things a lot easier to process.*>

<*Seriously? I feel like that makes it impossible.*>

<*OK, Jinx,*> Iris said in a more serious tone. <*You ready? Station sensors say that* ***nothing*** *is going on in there, so we know they're compromised. But it's a big space with a ton of equipment. Shooters could be hiding anywhere.*>

<*Ready to rock and roll.*>

A moment later, the doors slid open, and both AIs quickly advanced to take cover behind a large tank. Just as they hunkered down and began surveying the space, a rocket flew out and slammed into the deck a few meters behind them.

Iris got her drones out, and as they rose into the air, she picked up dozens of enemies. From the energy signatures, they were all armed to the teeth.

<*Well, shit, Jinx, I think this just might be the place.*>

<*And here I was hoping for a foot rub.*>

Iris signaled for the other AI to move to the far end of the tank while she sent out more drones to get a better view of their surroundings.

<*Hey, Jessica, you done playing with your pet crew on that ship?*>

<*Yeah, Trevor's bringing it in. I'm on the* Sexy.>

<*Good,*> Iris replied. <*There's an external airlock at the far end of this place. We're going to need help.*>

<*How much help?*>

<*Let's just say you should charge up.*>

UNLEASHED

STELLAR DATE: 05.11.8948 (Adjusted Years)

LOCATION: Unknown location, Cerka Station

REGION: Mullens, Virginis System, LoS Space

Consciousness eased its way back into Amanda's mind as she slowly became aware of her surroundings. She was laid on her back on a stiff feeling mattress.

With her eyes still closed and only feeling half awake, she tried to adjust her position to one that was a little more comfortable, but found she couldn't move.

Or, more accurately, her arms and legs couldn't move.

Amanda stopped trying to shift her position, and thought back to the last thing she remembered. A sinking feeling settled in her gut. She was wide awake now, her adrenaline beginning to pump, but she kept her eyes closed and her breathing calm.

Summoning her Magic she instinctually pulled on the Essentia she'd stored in her body, rather than on the ambient Essentia in the world around her, and noticed it flowed through her much easier.

She mentally smiled to herself.

Of course. That was the issue. Essentia didn't flow as easily here as it did back home. That would account for the strain she'd felt when she'd attempted to use more powerful Magic, but it only really became obvious as she siphoned the Essentia she stored inside herself and compared the flow.

She was relieved; this was something she could work around. She just needed to make a minor change to what she would normally do, and she'd be able to use her Magic unfettered.

She set her mind to begin multitasking, splitting it into more than a dozen separate minds linked to form a hive, with several of them constantly pulling Essentia into herself to store it like a battery. It was a simple thing to do and seemed to—at least so far—negate the issues she had been experiencing with her Magic use in this universe.

She conjured a second set of senses and placed them just above her prone body. Light flooded her mind as she looked around at the room through this Magical vision.

Her surroundings were small and dirty, made of grimy metal bulkheads, grated flooring, and bright white lights set into the ceiling.

She was laid out on some kind of medical bed that encased

her lower arms and legs in sturdy looking clamps with blinking lights on them. Sensors were attached to her head and body, which she noticed was currently naked. Her boots and suit were laid off to one side on a chair.

There were several robotic arms attached to the bed, hanging in the air above her, each one ending in fine needles that looked ready to slide into her.

The only other person in the room sat with his back to her, checking over what looked like more attachments for the robotic arms. To the man's left, a little closer to Amanda, was some kind of terminal, with a display that appeared to show her vitals.

The wires attached to my head and chest must feed into that machine.

"You can pretend you're asleep as much as you'd like, miss, but you can't fool us."

Amanda opened her eyes. "Apparently not," she replied.

The man turned to look at her.

He was young and surprisingly handsome, which threw Amanda for a moment. She'd expected some kind of monster.

She raised an eyebrow. "Hi there. I don't normally get naked on the first date, you'll have to forgive me," she said.

The man smiled. "Sorry about that, just making things a

little easier to work with. Also, we're going to need to take a look at that bodysuit of yours. It's got some curious properties that might be of interest to certain people."

"You could have just asked," Amanda replied.

The man smiled in a condescending manner. "Nice try. Now, speaking of tech, I have quite a bit of work to do on you," he said as a light on the console flashed.

With a whir of motors, the bed tilted up. She was propped in a more upright position, although not quite vertical.

"Me?" Amanda asked, choosing to play along. She wanted to see what these guys—whoever they were—wanted.

"But of course. You must be harboring some seriously advanced tech in that cute body of yours, miss. We saw you using some powerful personal shielding and stealth tech, and yet, our scans say you're a true-blue, all natural, vanilla human. So here we are.

"I'm going to dig around inside you and pull out whatever this advanced tech is. Might go for a pretty penny. Or maybe we can use it ourselves.... Can't be too careful, with all these AIs getting ideas above their station, you know."

"Is that right?"

Amanda used her Magic and dove into the man's mind, working carefully so as not to make him aware of her presence. She looked into the truth of what he was saying, only to be confronted with some incredibly grizzly memories of other people he'd worked over.

"I won't lie," he continued. "This is going to hurt. Quite a lot, actually. Should be fun though, yes?"

"Well," she replied nonchalantly, "as much as this sounds like a laugh a minute, I really am going to have to take a raincheck. I have other priorities right now, things to see and people to do, you know?"

"Cute," the man replied, as a light flickered on the console and the robot arms swung to life.

Amanda smiled and concentrated. With a snap of air, she Ported across the room, appearing right behind him.

"Wha—" the man exclaimed.

Amanda reached out and grabbed him, pulling him backward and throwing him against the wall with a thud. Stepping up to him, she caught him by the neck and squeezed.

"You know, that really wasn't a nice thing you were going to do to me."

The man gagged and clawed at her fingers in panic.

"The CPS are really going to want to speak to you, I think," she added, and slammed his head against the wall, knocking him out.

He dropped to the floor in a heap and lay still.

"Nighy-night."

With a last smile at the unconscious man, Amanda moved over to the chair holding her clothing. With another quick working of her will, her clothing snapped onto her body.

"That's better," she said to herself as she turned toward the door just as it slid open with a hiss.

On the other side, several armored men toting impressively large rifles opened fire on her. Rail-fired pellets streamed toward her, while a beam of light slashed across her body, burning into her Aegis, but not passing through it, leaving her unharmed.

"Boys," she scolded, shaking her head. "Is that any way to treat a guest?"

With a thought and a threatening step forward, she raised her hands, sending Magical lightning laced with Essentia and kinetic energy lashing out with a blinding flash and an ear-splitting *boom*.

Electronics fried, internal liquids violently evaporated, and the entire group was flung backward, as arcs of residual electricity snapped and popped around the metal room. Some of the men in the group had died instantly, but a couple of them moaned in agony as they clung to life.

Walking forward, Amanda spotted a corridor leading off from the room. She looked down it to see a man with a gun looking at her with an expression of horror. He blinked, and then turned and ran.

"No you don't," she muttered, and reached out, grabbing him telekinetically.

The man flew back into the room in a second. She held him above the ground with a magical grip on his neck, while he clawed at the invisible and insubstantial hand that gripped him, making it hard for him to breathe.

"Don't mind me, just need to check something," Amanda told him, and reached into the man's mind, hunting for anything that might hint at working with the Reavers—seeing things he couldn't explain, or any sign of Magic being used on him—but she found nothing.

What she did find were memories of some terrible actions that he and his fellow gang members had taken part in. Some of the images turned Amanda's stomach, and many of the victims had been entirely innocent.

She pulled out of his mind and looked up at him. "You disgust me."

"Who…who are you?"

"Judgment," Amanda said, and slammed his head into the

overhead, knocking him out. "The CPS is going to have a field day with you lot."

She released her magical hold of him and let his body drop as she strode out of the room, determined to put a serious dent in the abilities of the gang to hurt anyone else.

Walking up the corridor, she passed a series of doors on either side, and pushed her extra set of senses into the rooms beyond. They were cells, and half of them were occupied with people who were chained up and naked—or nearly so—and several of these looked malnourished.

"Fuckers," Amanda cursed.

She'd make sure these people were freed, but for now, they were safer in here.

The corridor ended ahead, opening out into a room. As she peered forward, she could hear shouting and the start of gunfire.

With a thought, she pushed her secondary senses into the large room, which was filled with more gang members readying weapons and charging through to the next room via large loading doors.

Amanda pushed her senses further, into the next room. It was a large space like the first, filled with pipes, machinery and walkways. She quickly spotted Iris and Jinx on the far side behind cover, firing at a group of thugs holed up around a cluster of pipes.

She smiled, though she wondered where Jessica was.

She shrugged off the thought and walked forward, readying her Magic as she went. As she reached the end of the corridor, a woman ran across her path and then spotted her. The thug skidded and fumbled with her gun, and Amanda hit her with a magical punch of energy and threw her the length of the room. She hit a thick pipe with dull *thud* and stopped moving.

That caught the attention of many already inside the room, and they watched their comrade fall, and then turned to look at Amanda, their eyes wide with shock.

Several of them then looked toward the middle of the room, where a man was standing by a table. Amanda recognized him as the guy who had been talking with the pirate Alma, and guessed he was likely the gang's current leader.

"You and I need to have words," she told him.

The man blinked twice as he looked at her, his aura betraying his shock through her Aetheric Sight.

"Don't just stand there, you idiots, kill her," he finally yelled, pulling his rifle from the table.

Gunfire filled the room with its staccato beat, the incredible noise bouncing off the walls and drowning out all other sounds.

With a working of her will, Amanda used the Essentia within her to send out a powerful shockwave of kinetic energy that washed over the room.

The men and women all around her were knocked off their feet, thrown black by the blast and sent flying, dropping to the floor, or smashing against machinery or pipes, and *then* falling down. The leader smacked into the table behind him and flew over the top of it, landing awkwardly on the other side.

The gunfire died away as the wave faded, leaving bodies strewn across the floor, moaning and groaning in pain as they crawled or tried to stand up.

Amanda started to cross the room toward the leader. To her right, a man raised his gun with a shaky hand. Lightning snapped from Amanda's hand and hit him with a loud *bang*. He dropped to the floor and stopped moving.

Ahead, a female gang member crawled away from Amanda, her ears bleeding from the shockwave, as she tried to reach the gun that had been knocked from her hand.

With a thought, Amanda hit her with a kinetic punch that knocked her out cold.

She could see the leader moving on the other side of the table, but couldn't see what he was doing. As she reached the table, Amanda hooked her fingers under the edge and threw it across the room with her enhanced strength, a good twenty meters.

Finally revealed, the leader turned his huge rifle on her and fired. The grenade shot toward her and exploded against her Aegis as a violent fireball that enveloped her in an orange and yellow glow.

The power of the blast knocked her back, even with her Aegis shedding most of the force from the pressure wave and protecting her from the intense heat. She regained her balance quickly, and with a sigh, advanced, quite aware what it would look like to her enemy to see her stride out of the explosion unhurt, her crimson hair billowing around her shoulders.

The look of utter shock on his face was a delight, as she reached out with her Magic and transformed the molecules that made up his gun and turned them into ash that drifted out of the man's hands. He watched it happen with greater fear.

"What the hell are you?" he gasped as he looked up at her.

"Your worst nightmare," she replied with a smile.

The man looked around, casting about desperately looking

for anything that could help him. He scrambled back from her as she advanced upon him.

Amanda reached into the man's mind and plucked his name from his memories, while also doing a quick hunt for any Reaver connections—though she didn't find any.

"Kirk," she said, and then smiled to herself. "No relation to James T., I take it?"

Kirk paused and looked confused.

"Forget it. I've dealt with your sort more times than I care to count. I've seen the cells you have back there—"

"Rival gang members," he blurted. "Killers, all of them…"

"Oh shut the feck up," she said with a sigh. "I've read your mind, I know exactly who's in those cells, and most of them are entirely innocent."

Kirk stared at her for a moment, and then jumped up, pulling a pistol from his boot as he rushed her, firing wildly.

She pulled on Essentia once more and conjured a violent build-up of pressure inside his head, which exploded in a shower of blood and brains. His body fell limply to the floor.

Cries of anger rose up from several places around the room, as the people who'd recovered somewhat from the shockwave raised their weapons.

They clearly haven't learned their lesson, she thought as they opened fire.

Lightning snapped once more, flashing out from Amanda's hands to hit these latest attackers and drop them all back to the floor.

She looked around her at the bodies that lay scattered about. Several of them were dead or dying; the rest were suffering from burns, broken bones, and other severe injuries. They should recover with medical aid, but they were incapacitated for now and would be easy for the CPS to pick up.

Amanda turned and walked toward the large, open loading door that led to the next room. Gunfire was still ringing out from within. As she walked, she hunted for the Link signal that she knew Iris and Jinx would be using. She found it and tapped into it.

~Hey, guys, want some help?~ she offered.

<*You're alright?*> Iris asked.

<*It's good to know you're alive,*> Jinx stated plainly.

~I'm fine, girls. Better than fine, actually. I think I'm finally getting used to this universe.~

<*That is a strange thing to say,*> Jinx replied.

~I guess. Did you guys come to find me?~

<*Of course,*> Iris replied. <*Jess thought you'd been kidnapped by*

one of the gangs you encountered.>

~She wasn't wrong,~ Amanda replied.

<Well, she's on her way. She should be here any moment…. Gah, these guys won't give up,> Iris exclaimed.

Walking into the back of the room, Amanda quickly spotted several gang members still up and shooting, alongside others who lay dead or dying on the ground, sporting wounds from weapons fire.

~I see you've been busy,~ Amanda commented.

<All in a day's work,> Iris replied.

<This is all still very new to me, but I think I'm getting the hang of it,> Jinx laughed nervously.

<You can say that again,> Iris replied.

<Um, okay. This is all still very new to—>

~It was a turn of phrase, Jinx. No need to actually repeat yourself,~ Amanda replied with mirth.

<Aaaah, I see, yes. Makes sense.>

~I'm coming through, I'll meet you in the middle,~ Amanda said as she strode in their direction.

As she moved, more lightning and kinetic rams snapped from her hands and smashed into the men she saw before her, dropping them to the floor in moments. Some turned and fired on her, their weapons being next to useless against her as she walked through the machinery toward an open area ahead. Through her Aetheric Sight, Amanda could see the life signs in the room, and watched as Iris and Jinx fired upon the last of them, finally taking out the final man with a precise beam shot to the head from Jinx.

~Good shooting,~ Amanda complimented her.

The two AIs stepped out from their cover and walked toward her, scanning the room as they approached.

"It appears we won the day," Jinx said.

"Looks that way. Jessica won't be happy that she missed out on all the fun," Iris added.

Amanda's powerful hearing picked out some distant gunfire that sounded like it was getting closer. "Don't be so sure," Amanda replied, causing Iris to frown.

"Oh, yes, I see what you mean," Iris said as she looked to Amanda's left.

Amanda followed the AI's gaze to a door with a small window set into it. As they watched, light strobed on the other side in time with the rapid bursts of gunfire. Several shots tore through the door, followed by a figure covered in blood who collapsed into the room.

As he fell, he revealed Jessica standing behind him, her rifle tucked over her shoulder.

She looked up and spotted her friends. “Damn, looks like I got here too late.”

“Better late than never,” Amanda replied with a smile.

“You seem brighter. Everything OK?” Jessica asked as she walked over.

“Fine now, yes. Feeling good. Sorry if I gave you a scare earlier, this universe has been messing with my Magic a bit.”

“You just disappeared,” she said accusingly

“I know. I blacked out. I was having issues using my Magic, but I’ve got a handle on it now.”

“Glad to hear it.”

<*Did you do all this?*> Jinx asked from behind her.

Amanda turned to see that the AI had walked across the room and was now at the other side, looking into the area where Kirk had been.

“Err, yeah, that was me,” Amanda replied a little sheepishly. She wondered if she’d taken things a little too far.

“Well, remind me never to get on the wrong side of you,” Jinx commented, as Iris and Jessica walked over to have a look themselves.

Jessica whistled in appreciation. “Stars, you took on a whole room?”

“They pissed me off,” she replied, feeling her cheeks flush.

"No kidding. Well, I'm glad you're on our side," Jessica replied.

"That reminds me," Amanda said, waving at the room before them, "we should call in the CPS to mop up."

"Already did," Jessica answered her. "They'll be here momentarily.

<*Jessica! we need you back here,*> Sabrina yelled through the Link. <*We've got—*>

The message cut out with a snap, and the ship disappeared from the station's network.

"Shit, sounds like trouble," Jessica said.

"Let's go," Amanda agreed, and worked her Magic, Porting the group across the station back to *Sabrina*.

THREATS

STELLAR DATE: 05.11.8948 (Adjusted Years)

LOCATION: ***Sabrina*****, Cerka Station**

REGION: Mullens, Virginis System, LoS Space

Sabrina watched everything going on with the utmost suspicion.

Despite liking Cerka and the people of the Virginis System, it was the place she and her crew had been attacked the most in their long years together.

At present, even though Jessica, Iris, and Jinx were off searching for Amanda, it was the events in the ship's main loading bay that had the bulk of her attention.

Cerka Station's police were bringing aboard five more bodies of Reavers that had been killed in a shootout at another military depot. That brought the total count of bodies stacked inside her hull to thirteen.

Thirteen more than she'd like to see.

<*I don't like this,*> she said on the ship's general network.

<*We know,*> Amavia replied from where she was examining one of the corpses in the medbay.

<*Oh boy do we know,*> Cheeky added. <*I don't like it either. I mean...what do we do with them when we're done?*>

<*Incinerate them,*> Usef said. <*If these people really are from another universe, then we don't need people buying and selling their remains for centuries. That's the sort of shit that starts wars.*>

Sabrina felt the same way, eyeing the final body as it was set on the deck next to Usef. He exchanged a few words with the CPS personnel as they turned to leave the ship, and the AI initiated a scan of the five sealed body bags.

They were a little warmer than room temperature, which was to be expected, given the fact that the people within had died only a short time ago.

For a moment, it looked as though one of the bags had moved, and Sabrina checked the replay, uncertain as to whether or not it was just a limb inside settling after being moved, or something else.

<*Usef, can you check the third ba—*>

Even as she sent the message, she watched the bag disintegrate and a man rise from the dust left behind. She immediately recognized him from the feeds in the bay on the lower ring as the man who had fought, and nearly bested, Amanda.

One of the things that Sabrina loved about being an AI—

especially an AI that had seen its core upgraded by none other than Earnest Redding—was that she was fast.

Blindingly fast.

Additionally, she was—and had always been—incredibly paranoid.

Ever since Sera had rescued her from a scrapyard, long decades ago, the AI had feared that her ship, and by extension, herself, would be captured and disabled, left derelict, or scrapped, or sent to some other terrible fate.

Stasis shields kept her safe on the outside, but much of the time, she was docked with questionable stations. She took comfort in the knowledge that she'd worked with her human crew to ensure that the ship's internal defenses were up to the task of repelling boarders.

A lot of boarders.

They'd never been put to the test against a magic-user—*if that's what these Magi really are*—but she was about to find out how well her weaponry and other tricks would do.

That was where her main advantage of speed came into play.

By the time the man had reached his feet and clamped a hand around Usef's neck, twenty-seven turrets had trained on him, six firing before a single word had left his lips.

If it hadn't been for Usef's proximity, she would have unleashed every beam she had on the enemy Magus, but that would have burned the Marine colonel to ash as well, so she dampened her fury to a dull scream of relativistic photons.

Light flared around her target, and he stumbled backward, losing his grip on Usef.

"Go!" the colonel screamed at the station police while running across the bay himself, pulling his helmet back on.

Sabrina watched her human crewmember move behind a crate that contained a grav generator that would shield him from any incoming weapons fire—though she didn't know what that would do against magic. His best bet, she suspected, was for her to keep the enemy distracted as long as possible with withering weapons fire from as many directions as possible.

"Fucking core!" Cheeky exclaimed as alerts lit up across the bridge. "You're gonna burn the bay to ash, Sabs."

<*I can live with that,*> the AI said while providing updates to Amavia and Misha, directing them to get armored up and ready for combat. <*You too, Cheeks. For all we know, one of those people could Port in here any second.*>

"Dammit," the pilot muttered as she dashed to the back of the bridge and backed into the emergency armor rack, letting it encase her in medium-weight ISF plating. "Just let them try me."

While conversing with Cheeky and advising the rest of the crew of their situation, Sabrina continued to hammer the Magus with beams, growing increasingly frustrated as his personal shield continued to hold.

Four other figures had also risen from their body bags, two dissolving them like the first Magi had, and two others cutting their way free.

<I think there are two more of these magic people,> she advised the crew, opening fire on the others, only to find that they were protected by shields as well.

<And two regular schmoes,> Usef added. *<Maybe you should switch to kinetics.>*

<I'm mixing them in,> Sabrina replied. *<You just can't see them in the haze. Going to try something new.>*

Normally, a-grav systems were very carefully limited to never exert more than one *g* of positive force, though they were capable of producing many, many times that.

When a ship was under heavy thrust, it could create internal forces as high as one hundred *g*s—easily enough to pancake a human, and much of the ship's interior as well. To ensure no overcompensation occurred as a ship maneuvered in space, the limiting factors on a-grav systems were considered sacrosanct and unmodifiable.

Sabrina didn't see it that way.

<*Hitting them with twenty* gs,> she warned. <*It shouldn't reach you, though, Usef.*>

Triggering the boost in artificial gravity had the desired effect. These new enemies may have amazing powers at their disposal, but they weren't prepared for their bodies to instantly weigh a few tons.

All five enemies hit the deck, and she could plainly see that two had bones protruding from their legs. Even so, the protective shield still held.

<*More company!*> Usef advised, turning his fire to the bay's doors.

Sabrina had been watching the fight on the dock, where a group of Reavers were attacking the departing CPS forces. She'd been unable to render aid because none of her firing angles were clear—though as more and more of the station police fell, those opened up, and she fired on the attackers outside the bay as well as within.

Her internal beams were starting to tax their focusing apparatuses, lenses heating up as the energies being funneled in an unending stream began to take their toll. Two of the beams shut down for emergency cooling, and three more were on the brink.

<*Sabrina….*> Usef's voice seemed like it was wavering. <*The deck is white-hot in here. With the a-grav you're running, it's going to buckle.*>

<*Iris and Jinx haven't found Amanda yet,*> Cheeky announced. <*Jessica is on her way to help them.*>

<*Usef is right,*> Sabrina said. <*This isn't going to hold them for long. I'm going to pull away from the station and vent.*>

<*I'll just shoot those bastards out on the dock,*> Usef said as he fired on several Reavers who were trying to enter the ship. <*But if you could close the—*>

<*I can't,*> Sabrina said, adding a few choice words after. <*Mechanism is jammed. Turning on the grav field.*>

For a moment, a grav field snapped on, sealing the ship from the dock, but then it disappeared, the emitters registering critical failures.

Then the grav emitters in the deck failed, and the first Magus who had risen from his body bag climbed back to his feet.

"Thanks for showing me how those work, ship. Don't mind if we just pop around your insides and see if we can't find what we came for."

A second later, the first man disappeared, and then the other two that she'd flagged as magic users winked out of existence as well.

<*Go!*> she ordered Usef, finishing off the two Reavers on the deck and then directing the full fury of her defenses against the enemies on the dock outside.

At the same time, she spotted the three Magi appearing in different places on the ship. The moment they popped into place, she boosted the a-grav, but they were ready for it and moved to a new location before the systems could deliver the crippling weight.

<*It's like playing whack-a-mole,*> she said a moment before one of the Magi appeared on the bridge.

It wasn't the first man, but rather one of the others—a tall, lanky woman—who strode toward the captain's chair, peering around.

Sabrina felt a sense of pride as Cheeky opened fire, not even throwing out a quip before a series of pulse blasts slammed into the woman.

The magic user was bowled over, but rose to her feet in an instant, turning to face Cheeky with a sour grimace on her lips.

"So, you wanna play?" she asked.

"I always want to play," the pilot replied, firing an electron beam that splashed harmlessly against the Magi's personal shield.

"Play with this," the Reaver hissed and lifted her hands, bolts of electricity leaping form her fingers and streaking toward Cheeky.

Sabrina was annoyed by the damage the energy did to some of the consoles, but her friend's ISF armor weathered the barrage without issue.

"That all you have?" Cheeky asked. "I have slug-throwers that pack more punch."

"What the…?" the Magi muttered, then shook her head and swung her right arm.

Sabrina didn't see anything leap across the space, but a moment later, there was an impact on the pilot's shoulder, and Cheeky dropped to a knee.

"Ouch!"

Without hesitating, Sabrina opened fire with a trio of electron beams, happy to see that this Magi's shield seemed to have trouble warding off her attack.

Although unable to see the force field directly, Sabrina could make out where her beams ended and the energy from them washed over the invisible field. She used this discovery to push her attack, and the Magi's shield faltered just enough for a beam to slip through and slice off her right hand.

A gasp of pain came from the Reaver's lips, and then Cheeky was right in front of her, lifting the woman off the ground and throwing her across the bridge.

<*Was that necessary, Cheeky?*> Sabrina asked.

<*Damn skippy it was. Is she out?*>

The AI scanned the woman. <*Yes, though I'm not sure for how long.*>

"Think they need their hands to do magic?" Cheeky asked as she approached the Magi.

<*Maybe?*>

A beam shot later, and the Reaver's other hand was gone.

"How's the rest of the ship?" Cheeky asked.

"Ship's OK. I'm not."

While Cheeky had been fighting the Magi on the bridge, the other two had continued moving around the ship until they both suddenly appeared in Sabrina's node chamber.

"So," the head Reaver said as he approached, eyeing the dozen turrets that had slid into place. "You know you can't defeat me. I can hold on until your weapons give out, then I win."

"Would you like a cookie?" Sabrina asked through the chamber's audible systems.

"Maybe later. What I want to know is where your stasis systems are located. I think I've just hopped through every room on this tub, and I can't find them."

"My what systems?" Sabrina asked. "You mean stasis pods? They're in Hold Six, one deck down."

"Don't toy with me, AI," the man said as he took a menacing step forward. "I can't see into your mind properly—it's all a jumbled mess—but I *can* threaten your body."

As he spoke, the ultra-hard, gold-titanium cylinder protecting her core began to slowly dissolve.

<Jessica! we need you back here,> Sabrina replied through the general channel. *<We've got—>*

"No you don't," the Reaver leader cut in.

She opened fire on the man, but his shield weathered the storm, and then her grav-emitters went offline again.

"Don't worry," he said in a soft voice. "This won't take too long."

<Help!> Sabrina wailed. *<Jessica?>*

CAVALRY

STELLAR DATE: 05.11.8948 (Adjusted Years)

LOCATION: *Sabrina*, Cerka Station

REGION: Mullens, Virginis System, LoS Space

Amanda snapped into existence on the bridge with Jessica, Iris and Jinx, appearing right beside Cheeky.

Cheeky yelped in surprise. "Stars, don't do that. I nearly shot you."

"Shit, that messes with my head," Jessica put a hand to her temple, then turned to the pilot. "Cheeks, where are they?"

"Everywhere! But I can't reach Sabs now…."

Amanda concentrated and looked around, focusing on Essentia, looking for knots of magical energy that would betray the location of the Reaver Magi. She saw three, one of them unconscious on the bridge, two meters away, and the other two a deck or two down, a little further aft.

"Got 'em," Amanda said, and Ported from the bridge to reappear in a ten-meter-square room in the heart of the ship.

She could sense the locus of energy in the complicated-looking device at the center of the room, noting the sentience held within. Magic, wielded by two figures standing on the other side of her, was slowly dissolving parts of its casing.

With a quick working of her power, Amanda conjured an Aegis, which snapped into place around what she guessed to be Sabrina's mind, cutting off the Reavers' Magic.

Simultaneously, she conjured another Aegis, a much bigger one, around herself and the other two Magi to keep them from Porting away and dragging this out for another few days. This would end today, right now!

This occupied only two out of her ten free hive minds. The rest, she set on the offensive to release a torrent of energy at the pair of Reavers.

Her Magic slammed against both of their personal Aegises with inexorable fury. White arcs of electrical energy flashed, pipes exploded, and the two figures hit the far wall, smashing through the door as her Magic tore through the surrounding bulkhead.

<Aaaaah, thank you, I thought that was the end for a moment there,> Sabrina said through the Link.

The Reaver who Amanda had briefly encountered in the attack on the lower ring weathered her initial blow much better than the other, and astoundingly landed on his feet in a crouch with one hand on the floor.

He looked up. "We meet again," he said as the other Reaver groaned, his Aegis flickering.

"You're not getting what you want," Amanda replied as she stalked over the twisted metal of the node chamber's entrance.

<*He wants the stasis shields,*> Sabrina cut in.

<*I knew it!*> Jessica shouted. <*Sure am glad to hear your voice, Sabs.*>

<*Glad you came to the party just in time for the main event,*> the AI replied. <*Get down here.*>

Cheeky snorted. <*Planet pushers couldn't keep us away.*>

"And you're going to stop me?" the Reaver sneered at Amanda.

"Yeh, damn skippy I am," she said with a smile.

Essentia flared from her, blinding light flashing out to smash into the prone Magus just behind the leader. His Aegis disintegrated as he spasmed and fell still, but he wasn't dead.

"Who are you? Who are you working for?" the Reaver asked. "Did Void send you? Has she been recruiting people?"

Amanda narrowed her eyes, not knowing if she should confirm or deny anything. Then movement behind the man caught her attention, as Cheeky slid down a ladder a dozen meters further down the passageway, followed by Jessica, Iris and Jinx.

~Take cover,~ Amanda suggested.

Cheeky crouched in a hatchway, while Jinx did likewise on the other side.

Jessica looked over at Amanda. *<I'll let you deal with this. Iris, with me. Usef and the others need help in the loading bay.>*

Then the purple woman was gone, running off down the corridor.

"I'm here because these guys are friends of mine. You picked the wrong feckin' day for a heist, my friend," Amanda answered her opponent, while Cheeky and Jinx moved around behind him.

"Morden," the other Magus croaked, reaching up toward the lead Magus.

"Shut your mouth," Morden replied, glancing down at the other man.

Amanda took that as her cue to attack, and unleashed hell, throwing Essentia-infused electrical, thermal, and kinetic energy at the Magus. The Essentia smashed into his Aegis like a wrecking ball, burning into it with unrelenting force. Electricity arced around the corridor, warping panels and cutting through conduit as Morden returned the attack, hitting Amanda with a blast of his own.

She staggered back a step from the force of it, and then, working one of her minds, Ported across the space and appeared beside him.

She lashed out, punching him with her Essentia-laced fist. His Aegis flared as she hit it while her fist briefly passed through to catch him in the face and knock him back. She followed it up with a kick to his sternum, and then another, but he caught the second one and threw her to the floor.

"Uff," Amanda grunted as she looked into the face of the injured and prone Magus who'd been assisting Morden.

He blinked at her. Amanda smiled and Ported, appearing a little further along the corridor.

~Light him up, girls,~ Amanda sent through the Link, as Morden roared in fury.

<*With pleasure,*> Cheeky replied.

Cheeky and Jinx fired their weapons, while Sabrina 's turrets unleashed hell. Amanda joined them, focusing all her minds on sending a raging torrent of Essentia at the Magus, with the intent of overloading his Aegis, which would allow the girls' weapons to burn Morden to a crisp.

The Reaver retaliated with a brief attack before suddenly Porting with a flare of Essentia. He appeared behind Jinx, still inside Amanda's Aegis, and energy flashed. Amanda countered the attack, but it still hit the AI and sent her sprawling across the floor before the man Ported.

Amanda sensed him behind her as he attacked again, blasting one of Sabrina's turrets.

"Feck this," Amanda cursed, and shrank the Aegis that contained herself and Morden.

He reacted instantly, Porting to stand right before her, and grabbed her by the throat, pushing her to the floor. Straddling her, he hit her with his other hand while Essentia strikes smashed against the Aegis that contained them both.

Amanda was dimly aware of Jinx and Cheeky moving closer and firing at Morden whenever they got a chance, as she and other Magus rolled around on the floor, their personal Aegises flaring and sparking as they interacted.

Amanda smashed her fist into the man's face and kneed him in the groin, trying to fight him off, until she got her feet under him and kicked outward.

He flew back and sideways and hit the bulkhead, where Cheeky, Jinx, and Sabrina were able to concentrate their fire on him.

He rolled sideways along the wall, dodging their gunfire and stepped out, turning to face them as his attacks on the Aegis that Amanda had contained him with finally broke through.

As the Aegis failed, Amanda felt Morden's voice in her mind, broadcasting his thoughts on an open Link.

~You win this round, Red,~ Morden hissed. *~I'll see you around. Have fun cleaning up.~*

Essentia flared, and Amanda sensed his Magic reach out to three places around her, and suddenly, Cheeky, Jinx, and Sabrina's last remaining turret in this section of corridor disappeared.

She glanced back at Morden, and he winked. Then his Magic flared again, and she sensed him drop out of the universe.

He was gone.

Amanda spun and looked back along the corridor as a yell sounded through the Link.

<Amanda, we're outside!> Jinx said, as Cheeky screamed over the Link.

Amanda Ported to Sabrina's hull, her Aegis protecting her from the ravages of space as she stared out into the blackness. She spotted them right away, their minds and Cheeky's life force showing up clearly in her Aetheric Sight.

With a thought, she reached out and Ported them away, back inside the ship, into the corridor they had just left.

She sighed. "Freaking hell," she muttered, briefly enjoying the view of Cerka Station all around her before concentrating and Porting back inside herself.

She snapped into being in the corridor to find Jinx and Cheeky sitting on the floor. Both looked up at Amanda.

~He's gone,~ she told them.

"Gone? Gone where?" Cheeky asked.

"Out of this universe. Looks like he's given up on his mission."

"So, we won?" Jinx asked.

Amanda looked down at Morden's Magi comrade still lying on the floor nearby. He looked back at them with a worried smile.

"Hi. Um…sorry?" he ventured, raising his hands.

"This will only take a moment," Amanda muttered, and pulled on the energy stored within her as she dove into the man's mind. She wanted to know as much about the Reavers as she could. She also wanted to know who else was left on Cerka.

The information on the Cerka forces was easy to find; it seemed that everyone the Reavers had brought with them was either on *Sabrina,* or attacking it from the dock. Also, half of the forces on the dock had been recruited at the station—gang members who had been well paid to cause havoc.

Further probing also confirmed that their target had indeed been the stasis shields on *Sabrina*.

The info this Magus had on the Reavers, however, was more limited. He was more like hired help, not in the inner circle of the group. He was a part of Morden's crew, but only Morden had contact with the core of the Reaver faction.

Still, he did have a few fascinating bits of info related to other missions he'd been on. She decided she'd review those memories later and withdrew from his mind.

"Nighty-night," she said, and with a tweaking of his mind, knocked him out.

"So, that's it? It's over?" Jinx asked.

"This part is," Amanda said, and then looked up at the ceiling. "How are the others doing out there, Sabrina?"

<They lost their will to continue the fight pretty quickly when Jessica and Iris joined in. Trevor returned as well, so we had them in a pincer. It looks like it's all over now.>

"Excellent," Amanda replied.

"So, what do we do with these guys?" Cheeky asked.

Amanda looked down at the prone Magus. "I have an idea about that," she said. "Meet me in the loading bay."

With a thought, she worked her Magic, and reached out to

both the Magus beside her and the one on the bridge. Essentia coalesced in on her, and with a snap, she appeared in the loading bay with the two unconscious Magi on the floor beside her.

Ahead, Jessica walked up the ramp arm in arm with Trevor, Iris behind them. Usef stood leaning against the wall beside Misha, who sat on a crate looking shell-shocked.

Amavia was outside at the bottom of the ramp, talking to a CPS agent, while other station security rounded up the survivors and began to deal with the dead.

"Stars above," Misha said, looking up at Amanda with his hand on his chest. "Do you have to do that? You scared the crap out of me."

Usef laughed. "You wanna talk about getting the crap scared out of you? You weren't in here when these damn Reavers started climbing out of body bags and hitting us."

"Yeah, alright, I think you win that one," Misha shrugged.

Amanda smiled. "Did they not hurt you?"

"Two of them appeared in the galley. That made me jump, I can tell you."

"They didn't do anything?"

Misha shook his head. "I'd just removed a batch of cookies from the oven, so I offered one to them, but they just disappeared again."

Amanda laughed. "They didn't want your cookies?"

<I offered them one as well,> Sabrina chimed in. *<They weren't interested.>*

"Everything okay out there?" Amanda turned and asked Jessica.

"All squared away," Jessica replied with a smile. "Trevor brought his big gun with him."

"I'll vouch for its size," Cheeky said, hopping through the hatchway into the hold.

"Ladies, ladies, don't fight. There's more than enough of me to go around."

"Yeah, well, I have my sights elsewhere," Cheeky replied, glancing over at Amanda with a wink.

Amanda blew her a kiss and looked back at Jessica as Cheeky beamed at her.

"The CPS are sorting it all out, dealing with the people who were recruited from the station. No idea what we'll do with these guys, though. Are those two Magi dead?"

Amanda shook her head. "I have an idea, though. Let's see if I can make this work."

She closed her eyes and focused on her universe and then on Void herself as she reached out with her mind to the Arch

Magus.

It took a moment, and more than a little effort, but it was certainly easier pushing back into her own universe than coming here.

With a rush of energy that flowed over her like a warm shower, a voice entered Amanda's head.

~How can I be of service?~ Void answered.

~I have some Reavers here, alive and dead. I wondered if you might want to bring them back to our universe?~

~That would be ideal. I shall join you momentarily,~ Void answered, and withdrew from her mind.

Amanda opened her eyes to see everyone in the ship and looking at her.

"So?" Jessica asked.

"One moment," she said, and watched the space around her through her Aetheric sight.

Seconds passed.

"Was something supposed to happen?" Usef asked, just as Amanda saw a sudden build-up of Essentia right before her, in the middle of the bay.

Suddenly, a burst of rippling, silver energy was floating in midair. It looked like an endless fractal of expanding liquid chrome constantly folding in on itself as waves of blue energy flowed off it.

The crew of *Sabrina* looked on with wide eyes as the fractal expanded over the next two seconds, and then collapsed down into the shape of a nude woman made from gleaming chrome.

The figure floated above the deck, her silvery hair rippling behind her head as if under water. She turned her glowing blue eyes on Amanda and smiled.

"Greetings, Amanda. I see you have been successful," Void said aloud in her soft, melodious voice with its odd pitching effect.

"Void. Thanks for coming. And yes, thanks to this crew, Reaver Morden has left this universe behind," Amanda replied.

Void turned and looked over the people assembled around her. "You have my gratitude, friends of Amanda. The Reavers are a scourge upon the multiverse. Your actions today will not be forgotten."

"Just trying to keep Cerka in one piece…which seems to be a losing battle," Jessica replied.

Void turned back to Amanda. "I shall remove these Reavers. Do you wish to return with me?"

Amanda smiled. "Not just yet, I have some unfinished business to attend to," she replied with a glance at Cheeky.

"Also, there's someone I want to see before I leave."

"As you wish. I shall see you soon," Void answered.

Her body collapsed back into the mind-bending fractal that defied three-dimensional space, and with a snap, it was gone—and so were the bodies of the Reavers.

Silence filled the bay as everyone stared at the spot that Void had just occupied.

"What in the name of the core damned demons was that?" Misha asked.

"Her name's Void," Amanda answered. "She's a Magus like me, but much older. I'm just over a thousand years old, but Void is probably over ten thousand, and she travels the multiverse."

"She looked like a…thing…" Misha said, waving his hands around in the air.

"The emissions from her were all over the place. Like she was made of everything and then nothing," Jinx said with a look of awe on her face.

"I won't pretend to know much about that," Amanda said. "But many of the truly ancient Magi often transcend the need for a human form, becoming something like living energy."

Amavia glanced at the others. "Sounds like an ascended being."

"Maybe the Magi are our universe's version of them," Amanda replied.

"Then I know of an AI you should meet," Amavia suggested.

Cheeky skipped over and grabbed Amanda's arm, pulling her in close. "Not yet, though, we need to chill out a bit after all that." She looked at her with her piercing blue eyes. "You'll stay the night at least, won't you?"

Amanda smiled back at the blonde. "How could I refuse an offer like that? Of course I will." She gave her a wink before addressing everyone else. "We've not really had much chance to just sit and chat, with all this Reaver shite going on. I want to know more about you guys…and who this AI is that you want me to meet, Amavia."

"His name's Bob, you'll like him," she replied.

"Also, he's with Tanis, so if you're paying her a visit, he won't be far away," Jessica replied.

<*I gotta ask, why does she keep calling us 'guys'?*> Sabrina asked in a mock whisper. <*Most of us are women.*>

"It's a colloquialism, Sabs," Cheeky said. "Surprised you didn't get that."

<*Was just trying to lighten the mood, everyone's being so sober.*>

Jessica sighed and leant against Trevor. "I need a drink,

anyone else?"

Everyone's hand went up.

<Umm…Jessica?> Sabrina asked. *<There's a CPS officer on the dock who wants to talk to you. General Hera has also requested a meeting, and Virginis's president wants to see you as well.>*

"Dammit," Jessica muttered as she looked at the crew. "Well, don't drink us dry before I get back."

DINNER

STELLAR DATE: 05.11.8948 (Adjusted Years)

LOCATION: *Sabrina*, Cerka Station

REGION: Mullens, Virginis System, LoS Space

An hour had passed by the time Jessica finally made it back to the ship, surprised to find Trevor waiting for her in the main bay.

"I thought you'd be up in the galley, downing our best scotch with our new friend," she said, sliding an arm around his waist as he leant over to kiss her.

"You know me," Trevor said when their lips parted. "Always work to do. Plus, I had to clear out the local stiffs—the ones that Amanda's silver friend left behind."

"Stars," Jessica muttered. "We have enough trouble on our plates without interuniversal heists being a thing. I kinda want to forget that this even happened."

"Well, we're going to be remembering until this is all patched up," Trevor swept his hand around the bay.

Jessica nodded, noting the offline turrets that were still extended, the half-melted section of decking, and the scorch marks on the bulkheads.

"What a mess."

"You're telling me," Trevor replied.

"Well, husband mine, that is tomorrow-crew's problem. Today-crew should eat, drink, and be merry."

"The rest of that saying isn't very cheerful."

Jessica shrugged. "Well, for us, we just have to change 'die' to 'fly'."

"Or 'make repairs'." Trevor winked.

"So inspiring."

The sounds of merriment reached them long before the couple even began to climb the ladder to the crew deck. Once at the entrance to the galley, Jessica stood with Trevor, soaking in the view for a minute.

Amanda, Cheeky, Usef, and Amavia were all playing a game of Snark on one end of the worn wooden table, while Jinx and one of Sabs' mobile frames were helping Misha prepare a meal. Finally, Iris was leaning against one of the bulkheads, hollering intermittent, especially unhelpful directions to both groups, and laughing at their mistakes and misfortunes.

"Since when did you become such a rabble-rouser, Iris?" Jessica finally asked, striding into the room.

"I've always been a troublemaker. Don't pretend otherwise."

"She got you into half the scrapes you've ever been in," Trevor added as he walked toward Misha. "Sad state of affairs when you have the AIs helping you cook, while the meat suits all play games," he told the other man.

" 'Help' is a very interesting word," Misha said, turning to regard Trevor with obvious relief. "More like training them on a skill that has no value, purely for their amusement."

"Let's not change the subject," Iris called out. "What scrapes did I get you into? I distinctly remember getting you *out* of a lot of scrapes."

Jessica gestured at herself. "If memory serves, you were the one who got me mixed up with RHY and saw me end up with purple skin—"

"Which was one of the best things that ever happened to you," Iris interjected.

"Well, you…"

"Got you out of RHY's research labs, saved you from Derrick—twice—saved you and Cheeky on Serenity, convinced you to do the right thing, which made our family and saved Star City, stopped RHY from blowing us up at the Perry Strait…. Should I go on?"

"She has a really good point," Trevor said. "Iris is pretty much responsible for all of our success. We should make her captain."

Jessica cocked an eyebrow. "Wow! Way to change your tune. Mighty thin ice for a man of your size."

"I wonder what happened to Derrick," Iris mused.

"Well, we paid for him to be sent to a prison," Cheeky said. "Hopefully that's what happened." She gave an involuntary shudder. "That guy had the creepiest grey skin."

"What's wrong with grey?" Iris asked with mock indignation.

"Everything," Jessica said. "Luckily, you're silver. Silver gets a pass."

During the rapid-fire exchange, Amanda had watched the crew with growing amusement. After Jessica's last statement, she laughed loudly while shaking her head.

"Sounds like you've lived through some interesting times. Cheeky said you've crewed this ship for thirty years?"

<Well, almost two hundred, if you count the ship's AI,> Sabrina said in a morose tone.

"Don't give us that schtick, Sabs," Cheeky said. "You're not that weak-willed AI anymore. Plus, you and I have been through a lot! Next to her, I'm senior in tenure," she said the last to Amanda.

"Maybe Sabrina should be captain, if she's been a part of this ship for so long. Who's next in seniority?" Amanda asked, looking around.

"I guess I am," Jessica replied. "Well, Iris and I signed on at the same time, of course. I should add that Sabrina does own the ship…. So there's that."

<That's right, you all serve at my pleasure,> Sabrina said with a mock cackle.

"OK…that's a bit unnerving. I guess I'm next," Trevor grunted. "Though I was sort of drafted. Join-or-die type of thing."

Amavia blurted out a laugh. "That's not how I heard the story. It was more 'stay where you are and you'll die'."

"So what is your story, Trevor? How did you end up on Sabs?" Amanda asked.

"Ah, memories…. I used to work security jobs on a station nearby, but I threw some fists in an underground fight club kinda deal. Jess ended up in the ring, fighting against me…"

"It was love at first punch," Jessica smirked, playfully hitting him in the ribs.

"I won't deny, I did enjoy getting my hands on you," Trevor grinned.

Jess rolled her eyes, but continued to smile.

"I was next after Trevor," Misha supplied. "The crew saved me from a pair of homicidal women out to kill me."

Amanda laughed.

"Then me," Usef grunted. "Though I'm not really crew, this is just a temporary assignment."

"Assigned by Tanis?" Amanda asked.

"Uh huh. I sometimes wonder what she signed me up for," he answered with a deadpan expression, as his gaze swept the room.

Cheeky snorted and threw a handful of nuts from the bowl on the table at the Marine. "If you had your way, you'd never leave us."

"As much as I love the glitter guns I installed in the captain's chair, I won't be here forever. Everything comes to an end," he replied with a shrug.

"Glitter guns? Hah! Why am I not surprised," Amanda said. "I'll make a note of that for the *Arkady*."

"Is that your ship?" Jinx asked.

Amanda nodded. "Yup. It's smaller than this and doesn't have an AI, but it's home. Well, one of my homes."

"I signed on shortly after Usef," Amavia said. "Teeechnically, since he isn't crew, that means came on ahead of him."

"Amanda, you're always ahead of me," he replied.

"Sorry, what?" Amanda asked. "How am I ahead of you?"

"He means me," Amavia replied. "I used to be two separate people, Amanda and Yolonda. Our minds got merged in an attack, and now we're Amavia. Sometimes," she glanced at Usef, eyes narrowing for emphasis, "Usef forgets that."

The big man only shrugged. "You look like Amanda, and I knew her for over a century. I feel like this is a forgivable offense."

"How did you get to 'Amavia' from Amanda and Yolanda?" Amanda asked.

"Evil AI attacked our brains, Yolanda took refuge in Amanda's mods and mind, and things kinda got mixed up. It's been an adjustment, but we're—I'm—getting used to it."

Amanda nodded, wide-eyed, and Amavia shrugged.

"Life from death, you know. That's how it is."

"Obviously I'm the newest," Jinx added in the brief silence that followed Usef's statement. "I've only been with the crew for a few weeks. Before that, I was a refugee, and before *that,* I ran the navigation computer in an AST ship."

"You 'ran' a computer?" Amanda asked. "That sounds a

little like overkill to me, and cruel."

Jinx nodded. "Well…the AST doesn't view AIs the same way as the League of Sentients—or my new friends here in the ISF. I lived in slavery in the AST. I barely even knew the outside world existed, beyond plots, vectors, and trajectories."

"That sounds horrific. The Sentient AIs in my universe have full rights throughout the Nexus. They're treated the same as people."

"What's your world like?" Jinx asked. "Is it like this? I imagine with magic, it must be plenty different."

"In some ways, yes. It's still the twenty-first century where I'm from—2017, to be precise—but the Magi first traveled to space over ten thousand years ago and built their civilization in the stars. We call that the Nexus. Earth has been left to develop on its own for that entire time. The people there have no idea about the Nexus, although we came close to exposure when the dragons attacked New York this year."

"Dragons?" Cheeky asked, her eyes wide.

"You're kidding," Jessica said.

"And the weirdness returns," Misha muttered from beside the stove.

Amanda smiled. "No, I'm not kidding. They're called Void Dragons. They're magical creatures that fly through space.

Nasty feckin' things, too. Not easy to kill."

"Stars," Jessica muttered, shaking her head as she imagined having to fight off dragons.

"There's some on our side too. Got to ride one once, through the clouds of Jupiter."

"Wow, I'm totally jealous right now," Cheeky said. "I'm no dragon, but maybe you'd still be interested in a ride," she proposed with a wink.

Misha cleared his throat at that. "OK, glad everyone has talked themselves hoarse while I kept cooking, but I guess I'll share the food with you anyway."

<*It* ***is*** *your job,*> Sabrina chided.

"Whatever," the cook said with a laugh that was far happier than his words. "Not enough room on the table for all this, so everyone, grab a plate and go down the line. We've got steak tips, a lasagna-like dish—I had to improvise on the noodles—baked haddock, fries, potatoes six ways from Sunday, lots of greens to pick from, and the ribs I started earlier came out perfectly."

"Excellent, I've been looking forward to this. I'm famished," Amanda said as she rose with a smile. "Looks like a meal fit for a king."

"Or a starship captain," Jessica amended as she got in place behind their guest.

The crew loaded up on food and continued to swap stories for several hours, adding beer, wine, ice cream, and several other pastries to the ongoing meal.

Jessica noticed Jinx sitting and talking to Amanda about her universe in greater detail as they ate. The AI was sounding rather wistful, and Jessica wondered if she might decide to ship out.

Later, a dozen games of Snark were played. Amanda was given her own deck before Usef finally called it a night, followed by Misha not long after.

Jessica was feeling like she could use a half hour in Virginis's glorious sunlight before getting some shut-eye, when she noticed that Cheeky was making eyes at Amanda.

<*Are you demure?*> she asked the pilot privately.

<*A bit…I don't know if she's receptive, but there's no way I'm going to pass up the opportunity to have sex with someone from another* ***universe****.*>

Jessica couldn't argue with that logic. If she wasn't tired, and wasn't getting a vibe from Trevor that he wanted some time with her alone, she might have considered joining in.

<*So what's with you being so circuitous in your advances?*>

<*Stars, Jess, she's a sorceress. She could turn me into a newt.*>

<Funny, Cheeks. Magus. She's a Magus.>

The pilot sent a mental snort. *<Semantics. OK, look. Amavaia's getting ready to go, then it will just be Amanda, me and Iris. Smaller group, easier to flirt. So skedaddle.>*

Jessica and Trevor bade their farewells shortly after Amavia did, and they were barely in the passageway when Jessica clearly overheard Cheeky say, "OK, so where do you want to bang?"

"Doesn't waste any time," Trevor said, shoulders heaving in soft laughter.

"No, she sure doesn't. So long as she doesn't do it in the captain's chair, I don't care where they have sex."

This time, Trevor didn't hold back his laughter. "What about on the galley table?"

"Trevor! There are some things you just don't do! That's an antique!"

MOVING ON

STELLAR DATE: 05.12.8948 (Adjusted Years)

LOCATION: *Sabrina*, Cerka Station

REGION: Mullens, Virginis System, LoS Space

Amanda sat up in bed, leaning back against the headboard. She had just awoken from a long night's rest after what must have been a couple hours of bedroom Olympics with Cheeky. The pilot lay beside her, as naked as the day she was born, arms and legs splayed wide, breaths heavy and deep. She'd been insatiable, with a stamina that kept her going and going.

Amanda smiled at the sight of her. She was looking forward to getting home and telling Maria about her adventure and this pretty blonde. She'd likely be jealous.

After the stress of the last day, hunting down the Reavers and dealing with her issues using Magic, it'd been a much-needed release to just sit and enjoy the company of the crew for a few hours and get to know some remarkable people.

They were clearly close, and in many ways, a family. That bond was their strength and would see them through anything their universe could throw at them.

She felt glad to have found them, as she was not sure she would have been able to locate and stop the Reavers without their help.

But all good things come to an end.

As much as she'd love to stay a while longer, she knew she couldn't. She needed to get back home, but not before stopping by and seeing Tanis.

She'd put a fair bit of thought into the prospect over the last day, and there really was only one way to make it happen, given how this universe worked. She needed a ship.

Tanis was a long way off, but Amanda was determined to see this through. She wasn't sure when she'd be able to return here, and she wasn't about to head home without at least trying to see her friend.

Using her Aetheric Sight, she could see the crew in other parts of the ship. Many of them were already up and moving around.

With a last glance at Cheeky and a smile to herself, Amanda climbed off the bed and made her way to the shower. She'd not been in it long when Cheeky appeared around the corner with a smile on her face.

"Room for one more?" the pilot asked.

*****

Amanda sliced off another portion of sausage and skewered it with her fork before placing it into her mouth. Misha had cooked an excellent breakfast, and now stood leaning against the stove.

"So, how long are you going to be staying here for?" he asked, his tone abrupt.

Amanda laughed and Cheeky looked up at him. "Don't be so rude," she admonished.

"Hey, just asking," Misha replied, raising his hands in defeat.

"It's fine," Amanda smiled. "Don't worry, I'll be out of your hair today I think. I'm determined to try and visit Tanis."

"How are you going to do that?" Cheeky asked.

Amanda smiled. "In my universe, the Magi travel the stars in vessels we call Aether Ships. Basically, they're magical starships—"

"Are you going to Magic one from thin air?" Jessica asked, walking into the room.

"Pretty much," Amanda replied. "I'm going to need a space to do it in, though, like a docking bay or something."

"I'm sure we can arrange a loading bay. Sabs?"

<Sure, I'll get on it. Only if I get to watch, though.>

"Do you mean to say you weren't watching us last night?" Cheeky asked.

<Well, you were hard to miss. That's not what I meant, though. I was talking about–>

"I know what you meant," Amanda smirked. "And yes, you can watch. You can all watch me do it."

"Speaking of 'doing it', did you have a good night?" Jessica asked. "I could hear you and Cheeks all the way across the ship."

Amanda laughed. "It was a very pleasurable evening, thank you."

"Shame you couldn't join us," Cheeky added with a wicked smile.

"Maybe another time. My man needed some attention," Jessica replied.

Amanda smiled, loving the open and uninhibited nature of the crew. She wondered if it was like this everywhere throughout human space in the universe.

"He could have joined in too," she shrugged. "The more the merrier."

"I see that some of Cheeky's nature has rubbed off on you," Jessica commented.

"Not really, there were other things of Cheeky's that rubbed off on me though."

"Too much information," Misha exclaimed, looking flustered, much to the amusement of the girls.

<*I've booked a docking bay,*> Sabrina said.

"Excellent, thank you," Amanda replied. "Are we able to disable any security cameras in there?"

<*Shouldn't be an issue, I'll arrange it,*> Sabrina said as Jinx walked into the room.

"Good morning," Jinx said, greeting everyone and moving to sit beside Amanda.

"Careful, Jinx, you've entered the innuendo zone," Misha said in mock warning.

"Morning," Amanda said to the AI.

She'd enjoyed talking to Jinx the night before; the AI had chatted with her for a while, asking about her universe and what it was like there. She'd seemed genuinely interested, and Amanda had enjoyed explaining it to her.

"I've been processing everything we talked about last night, and I wanted to put something forward for you to consider," Jinx said.

Amanda nodded. "Sure. What is it?"

"I explained to you about how I have spent most of my life

inside a navigational computer. It was only by the aid of people like the crew of *Sabrina* that I am free and here today." She turned her attention to Jessica. "I am eternally grateful for everything you guys have done for me, but I feel like I need a fresh start, somewhere else." She focused again on Amanda. "Which brings be back to you. I am fascinated by what you described to me about your universe—it sounds like an incredible place. So I was wondering if you might consider taking me back with you?"

"Oh, wow. Okay," Amanda replied, a little surprised by the request. "Um, I'm not sure—"

"I of course would understand if you would prefer not to, or if there are restrictions about this kind of thing that I am unaware of," Jinx said.

"Are you sure about this?" Jessica asked, concern in her voice.

"I spent much of the night going through this, and spoke to Sabrina and Iris about it too," the AI told her.

<*She did,*> Sabrina confirmed.

"And you think this is a good idea?" Jessica asked the ship's AI.

<I can't see it doing any harm. Jinx has spent her entire life, apart from the last few weeks, embedded in a navigation system. Even for

AIs, that's going to leave an impression.>

"I will not go back to that life." Jinx's tone was steely.

<*I believe she needs to get away from Virginis. The further, the better,*> Sabrina said plainly.

"Well, you can't get much further than another universe," Cheeky commented.

Amanda nodded, thinking through the implications of what this would mean.

There were AIs in the Nexus, so it wouldn't be as if she were bringing anything truly unique over, and there were plenty of others crossing between universes it seemed, so an AI shouldn't make too much of a difference. She wasn't sure how Void would feel about it, but she honestly couldn't see it being too much of an issue.

"So, what do you think?" Jinx asked, looking up at her with hopeful eyes.

Amanda nodded. "I think we can work this out. I'm going to say yes," she replied.

A huge grin spread across Jinx's face.

"Thank you," she exclaimed, and pulled Amanda into a hug.

*****

"Alright, here we are," Jessica said, leading the group into a nearby docking bay, complete with large airlock doors that took up almost all of the far wall.

Amanda admired the space as she entered. There were a few crates along one side, but it was otherwise empty and perfect for her needs.

"So, what happens now?" Jessica asked.

Amanda turned away from admiring the room and looked back at the purple woman and the rest of the crew.

"Well, if you want to hang around, I just need some space and no interruptions for a little while. It shouldn't take too long."

Jessica smiled and nodded. "We can do that."

"Are you sure?" Trevor asked.

"We're not exactly known for our stoicism," Cheeky added.

"Okay, okay. Stars, you guys," Jessica said. "Private Link chatter only until Red says otherwise."

"Cheers, guys," Amanda said with a smile. Then she stepped away from the group.

They fell silent. Amanda could see the Link communication between them intensify, but she ignored it as she faced the room. Picking a spot, she sat down on the deck and crossed her legs. She closed her eyes and used her Magic to slowly draw in Essentia from all around her, being careful not to pull it in too fast and strain herself again.

In her mind, she began to visualize a ship. A small ship that could sleep maybe four people on bunks…something just big enough for her and Jinx to live in for a little while as they made their way to where Tanis was.

She envisioned a sleek, chrome vessel with red markings on it, and held that image in her head as she pulled on the Essentia within her and shaped it into the form of the ship.

She thought through the inside space and how it would be laid out, as well as the inner workings of it—which were minimal, given that it was powered, like all Aetheric ships, by a Magical core rather than an engine, an item imbued with certain enchantments that moved the ship.

In this case, a red oval gemstone in the main console.

She was unsure how much time had passed as she looked over the ship in her mind one last time, making sure everything was as it should be before infusing it with the last bit of Essentia needed to finalize the design.

Pleased with her vision, she opened her eyes and looked up to see a gleaming white chrome ship with red markings, hovering a meter above the ground in the middle of the bay.

With a smile, she sent a command to the ship's core, and the main boarding ramp levered open with a swift, silent motion.

"That was…awesome!" Cheeky said out loud.

Amanda blinked, her acute time sense telling her she'd been at this for a couple of hours. She stood up and turned around to face the crew, who had made themselves comfortable as they'd watched the ship form from nothing.

"That was impressive," Jessica agreed. "Nice design, too."

"Thanks," Amanda replied. "Now that I have my ride, I really should be going."

Jessica stepped forward and offered her hand. "Thanks for an entertaining couple of days, it's been wild."

Amanda shook her hand, and then pulled her in for a hug. "My pleasure. Hopefully it's not been too crazy."

"Just crazy enough, I think," Jessica laughed.

Amanda smiled. "Take care of yourself." She turned to Cheeky and embraced the pretty blonde. "Come here, you. Thanks for everything."

"My pleasure. It's been amazing. If you're ever back in our neck of the woods, feel free to drop by and say hello. I'll keep my bunk warm for you."

Amanda winked at her as she pulled back. "I'll bear that in

mind."

She went down the line, shaking hands with or hugging the rest of the crew, saying farewell.

"Thanks, Sabs. Hopefully I didn't leave too much of a mess behind," she said.

"Nothing we can't fix, just glad we could help," Sabrina replied, her mobile frame smiling back at her. "Maybe we'll meet again sometime."

"Just don't bring any dragons, if you come again," Misha added.

Amanda smirked. "I'll try not to." She turned to Jinx and smiled. "So, you still want to do this?"

The AI nodded. "I do."

"Then let's go."

Amanda waited as Jinx said her own goodbyes, then with a final wave, they boarded the ship. Amanda Linked her mind with the core, and an Aegis snapped into place around the ship as the ramp closed.

<Airlock door's opening,> Sabrina reported over the Link. *<Here's everything you need to know about New Caanan and where to find Tanis. Good luck.>*

Information flooded through the Link. She took the coordinates of the system and fed them into the core so it could plot a course. She could see the a-grav shield that held the atmosphere inside the open docking bay doors, and she slowly eased the ship out through it, into the void of space.

Through her Link to the ship, Amanda could see the crew of *Sabrina* standing in the hangar bay, watching the ship as she moved away from the station. With a smile, she fired up the ship's Flux Drive and jumped to warp, knowing that Jessica and the others would only see the ship suddenly streak away into the black and disappear from view.

*****

Amanda sat in the command chair on the bridge of the Aether Ship, watching as the countdown on the screen grew closer to zero, and hoping the ship would drop out of warp precisely where they needed to be.

It had been a sedate few weeks, as the craft barreled through space at speeds that Amanda found almost impossible to fathom— even so, she had managed to use her Magic to give them a boost and bring the travel time down a little. She had spent her free time resting, getting to know Jinx better, swapping information about each other's universes, and playing a few games…including Snark.

She wondered if a few weeks in this universe would translate to a few weeks in her own, or if the timestreams were different. Maybe they moved at a different speed? It would be something to look at another time, she thought.

Bringing her attention back to the HUD on the main screen, the numbers on the countdown reached single figures, and then finally hit zero, and the ship dropped out of warp. A planet shot out of the darkness to fill the viewer as they slowed to a more sedate speed, and Amanda stood up to get a better view.

"Wow, pretty awesome, huh? I wonder if this is where Tanis lives."

"From the charts Sabrina gave me, that's Carthage," Jinx replied. "And stars above, that's a lot of ships."

Amanda nodded mutely as she looked at the display of space around the planet. There were so many vessels that the individual markers formed a solid mass.

"How many are there?"

"Ummm…" Jinx tilted her head for a moment, then glanced at Amanda. "Close to a quarter million…though it's really hard to say, since so much of what is out there is debris from the battle Jessica told us about."

"Any sign of Tanis's ship?" Amanda asked.

"Nothing yet," Jinx answered.

"And we've not been detected?"

"No, I don't think so. I'm not seeing anything suspicious," Jinx replied.

Amanda nodded in satisfaction. She'd guessed that it would be a little dangerous for an unknown ship to suddenly appear insystem, so she'd built several enchantments into the Aegis that would render them invisible to both passive and active scan systems until they were able to find Tanis and Bob.

Amavia believed, given her long history with both Bob and Tanis, that the admiral would most likely be on the *I2,* Bob's ship, and have told the AI about Amanda's arrival in this universe.

"Just be careful where you fly," Jinx warned her now. "There's stuff *everywhere* out here. It's going to take them forever to clean this mess up."

"This shite is all over the shop," Amanda agreed.

Using the core, she urged the ship on and boosted closer to the planet, scanning the area for any trace of the *I2*. She'd assumed such a huge ship would be easy to spot, but with so many other engines flaring brightly as various craft worked to clear the debris, it was hard to find any sign of their quarry.

After half an hour, they finally caught sight of the massive craft as it came around the far side of the planet, high up in a geosynchronous orbit.

Amanda set a course and eased their ship toward it, taking care not to disturb any debris that was likely being tracked by monitoring systems.

"How close should we get?" Jinx asked as they closed to within one hundred thousand kilometers of the ship. "Wow…that thing is over thirty-six kilometers long! It's gotta be bigger than a whole battle fleet."

Amanda nodded absently as she considered her options. "I think for now we should stop here, and I'll Port over to find Bob."

"Good luck."

"Thanks."

The Magus conjured a second set of senses close to the huge ship and looked it over, hunting for something that mirrored Sabrina's node. The AIs aboard *Sabrina* had informed her that Bob's would be similar—though much larger, as he was a multi-nodal AI, and comprised of several AI cores linked together throughout the ship.

She grunted in surprise on seeing thousands of AI nodes, spread throughout the ship. So, not so straight forward after all.

She was quickly able to sort out the ones that were paired with humans, and the ones in mobile frames, such as Jinx and Iris. Once those were filtered from her view, there were still hundreds of AI nodes embedded through the ship.

Then she noticed a cluster standing out very brightly against the others, the interconnectivity between them far more complex than anything she'd seen so far.

One of the nodes rested in the center of the forward section of the ship. She made her choice. Concentrating, Amanda Ported, appearing inside.

"Hey, Bob."

A SURPRISE GUEST

STELLAR DATE: 06.02.8948 (Adjusted Years)

LOCATION: ISS *I2*

REGION: Carthage, New Canaan System

Bob watched the space surrounding the *I2* with an intensity few could match.

Too many fleets had gotten too close to the worlds of New Canaan for him to trust that the Intrepid Space Force could detect them before an attack commenced.

And so he watched.

At present, the multi-nodal AI was observing a periodic disturbance roughly one hundred thousand kilometers off the *I2*'s bow. It wasn't visible on normal EM bands, but that was not the boundary of Bob's vision.

In extradimensional space, there was a definite flicker of energy. Something he had been expecting to see for some time; an encounter that he didn't expect to be convivial.

The energy surge flared brighter, and then was gone. Fourteen nanoseconds passed in which he searched earnestly for its new location, when suddenly, a surge of extradimensional energy registered in his primary node.

A woman stood on the catwalk surrounding it. She was short, wore a white shipsuit with no insignia, and had long, red hair. This assessment was made in the space of twenty-two microseconds.

The lack of a helmet ruled out her being a human infiltrator—in his experience, humans were unlikely to expose their heads in dangerous situations.

The only other possibility is that she is one of the core AIs.

A millisecond had passed between when the woman appeared and when he arrived at this conclusion, which was estimated with only seventy-one percent certainty, but that was more than enough for him to snap a stasis field into place, encasing her in a solid bubble that burned away part of the deck in a brilliant flare, before the grav field lifted it in the air and surrounded it with vacuum to keep stray atoms in the air from impacting the stasis field.

At this point, two seconds had passed, and he disabled a part of the field off for several milliseconds over the span of a few seconds, gathering readings on the woman—or whatever she was—within.

What he saw surprised him in a way that nothing had in a very long time.

The stasis field he had initiated should have been a full bubble, making the woman within entirely immobile, but she was *moving*.

Carefully reading her lips, he saw her mouth the words, 'Hey, Bob'. Then her mouth became a thin line.

He carefully reviewed the stasis field's configuration. It should have functioned properly, but it was not drawing the correct amount of power. He attempted to retune the emitters, but when he flickered the field again, he saw that she was still able to move inside, and was saying something new.

"What the… Hey, now. Come on, Bob, let me out. That's cheating."

<Tanis,> he reached out to the admiral. She was having a celebration for her daughter, who was pairing with her other daughter, but he knew this was worth the interruption. *<I have an intruder in my primary node.>*

<I'm on my way.> Her response came in seconds. *<I'll be there in five.>*

<Good. Here is an image of her.>

Bob passed an image of the redheaded woman to Tanis, and a moment later, a laugh came back to him.

<Well, shit…that looks like Amanda.>

<Amanda?>

Bob knew several thousand people who bore that name. None of them looked like the woman he held in the field.

<*Remember that place I got sucked into? The one with the interdimensional bar,*> Tanis prompted.

<*I recall,*> he replied. <*I still wonder if it was an elaborate ruse.*>

<*I was there, too,*> Angela joined in the conversation. <*I've been in enough sims to know it was real. I agree with Tanis that this intruder looks like Amanda.*>

<*But hold her in the field till we arrive,*> Tanis added.

<*I had no other plan,*> Bob assured her. <*I've summoned a squad of Marines as well. However, I'll have them wait in the corridor outside. I think she might be an ascended being.*>

<*Or a sorceress,*> Tanis countered with a wry laugh.

Bob gave a courteous cough to show his displeasure with such nonsense. <*There is no such thing.*>

To his surprise, Angela laughed. <*Well, insofar as her abilities are concerned, pretend there is.*>

His conversation with Tanis and Angela had only taken a few seconds. Next, he summoned a holoimage displaying only the word 'Wait', and flickered it in front of the field for the woman within to see.

A second later, she was out of the field, a few meters away, glaring at him under lowered brows while raising a finger like an angry parent.

"Now that wasn't very—"

Bob snapped a new field around her and debated any further communication. He decided it was worth an attempt in an effort to get her to wait peacefully for Tanis to arrive. He moved the holodisplay, showing a new phrase.

'Tanis is coming. Please stop.'

The intruder suddenly appeared further down the catwalk.

"Look, Bob, I can do this all day."

"So can I," he replied, and snapped a new field around her.

This time when he checked, she was not inside.

Moments later, she reappeared on the far side of his node.

"Bob, please. I don't mean you any harm, and this is wearing a little thin."

"Then stop fighting it," he demanded. "The stasis field won't hurt you."

"You don't know that," she countered. "I'm from another universe.... What if it *does* hurt me?"

He waited a few seconds before replying; not that he needed to, he just found that it was useful to convey a sense of disbelief to humans.

"That is unlikely. If your universe was *that* different, then the laws of physics would have diverged enough that you would not have survived coming here. Your body would have been destroyed or dissolved."

"Fair point, well made," the woman replied.

"Our universe is mostly made of matter," Bob continued, "with very little antimatter. Imagine if you were to travel to a universe made of antimatter and not matter? You would instantly explode."

"Well, obviously. Are you messing with me?"

"I am not," Bob replied. "However, I suppose if you and Tanis really did meet in some extrauniversal bar, it is safe to assume that you're both made of the same type of matter. That being said, it's also probable that anyone who can create an extrauniversal space and bring people to it could have a way to ensure that different types of matter do not come in contact with one another."

A smile formed on Amanda's lips, crinkling the corners of her eyes. "Do you always talk like this?"

Bob had noticed that, though he could not detect EM emissions from her, Amanda had managed to tap into the ship's public network.

Rather than replying aloud, he backtraced her Link to reply.

<*No,*> he spoke in her mind. <*Normally, I talk like this.*>

Amanda's eyes widened, and a grin split her face. "Hah, wow, what a voice! Feels like I'm sitting on a bass speaker. Do it again."

<I do not perform at your pleasure, young lady.>

"Oooh, that felt good. You can call me Amanda, by the way."

<As you wish.>

"You know, speaking of exotic energy, you're not just any old AI, are you? I can see some curious energies around you that you seem to be affecting. But, you're not a Magus, are you, which leaves only one alternative…"

*****

Tanis managed to reach Bob's primary node only four and a half minutes after racing out of her lakehouse.

At times, she had half a mind to place a maglev line beneath her home, but hated the fact that it would decrease the number of walks she got to take through her woods. And that it might get her more visitors.

That thought was still filtering out of her mind as she nodded to the Marines stationed outside of Bob's primary node—all of whom appeared more relaxed than she expected—and then burst in to see Amanda leaning on the catwalk's railing, laughing and shaking her head.

"Shit! It *is* you, Amanda," Tanis exclaimed.

<Either that, or she's an ascended AI that has taken over Bob,> Angela commented.

<Unlikely,> Bob replied. *<If I had lost a fight, you'd see evidence…such as this ship no longer being here.>*

"He's a pretty serious guy," Amanda jerked a thumb toward Bob's node while winking.

"It's better than when he jokes," Tanis replied as she strode forward. The two women embraced while Bob made a sound of displeasure.

<I have it on good authority that my jokes are funny,> the AI said.

"Whose authority?" Tanis asked. "Angela doesn't count. You know she's messing with you half the time."

<Tanis! You wound me,> Angela said in a mock-shocked voice.

The two women separated, and Amanda spoke while looking around the chamber.

"This is one hell of a ship, Tanis. It's feckin' huge!"

"It's a nice place to call home," Tanis replied amicably. "Well, my home away from home."

"You normally live on the planet below?" Amanda asked.

"Recently, yes, though I've spent most of my life inside this hull."

Amanda's brow's lowered. "Oh really? So, it's not just a warship, then?"

Tanis tapped a finger on her chin. "No. It used to be a colony vessel—spent about one hundred and forty years in that state, give or take a bit of temporal distortion."

"Shite, that's a hell of a stretch."

"Well," Tanis paused. "You mentioned that you lived in New York once, right?"

"To be sure."

"OK," Tanis said as she turned to guide Amanda out of Bob's primary node chamber. "The interior of this ship, if you were to lay all the decks side-by-side, is the size of the old New York state. Lotta room to move around."

<*She loves to show off her home,*> Angela commented. <*You're going to get the full tour now.*>

Amanda nodded appreciatively. "Plenty of room to stretch your legs, then. But what about the green, green pastures of home? Or somewhere to catch some rays? Not that this pasty ass of mine gets much of that, but I'd miss the great outdoors a little, to be honest."

"Stars, yeah, me too."

"Remind me to take you to a little place I call Inisfail sometime," Amanda answered with a smile.

Tanis walked out into the corridor, where the squad of Marines still waited. "Sergeant, thanks for getting here so fast. Turns out it was just a little prank. You're dismissed."

The Marine gave Amanda a judging look, then nodded. "Understood, Admiral Richards." He turned to the twelve men and women lining the corridor. "Fall out, Marines!"

"Sorry, guys, just little ol' me," Amanda added with a smile and a wave to the sergeant.

Tanis led Amanda through the forward section of the *I2* to the central administrative corridor, describing some of the features as they went. When they came to the corridor—which stretched for half a kilometer between the bridge and the maglev terminal—Amanda shook her head in wonder.

"Tanis…this isn't a corridor, this is a feckin' street. Your starship has *streets* inside of it."

"Sure," the woman shrugged and gave a wink. "But we're on a ship, so it's a corridor, or a concourse."

"Yeh, right. That guy's workstation is bigger than my house."

Tanis placed a hand on Amanda's back and guided her

toward the avatar's foyer. "Just wait till you see this place."

They reached the forward end of the admin corridor, and two wide doors slid aside to admit them. The chamber beyond was thirty meters by sixty meters, and filled with dancing lights and holodisplays drifting through the air. At the center of it stood the avatar currently on duty, Priscilla.

She was fused to the plinth in the center of the room, long, wiry hair flowing out around her head, dancing to some music only she could hear.

As they approached, she swiped a hand, clearing the displays in front of her, and gave the two women a winning smile.

"Well, then, so you're the one who gave Bob a shock," she said in greeting.

<I was not shocked. It was just an unexpected visit.>

Priscilla's laugh sounded like icicles crackling when hit with sunlight on a cold winter's day. "You forget, Bob, I'm inside your head."

"Interesting. I can see the connection," Amanda said.

"You can *see* it?" Pricilla asked.

Amanda nodded with a smile. "I can see your thoughts blending with his, and his with yours. Oh, and yeah, he was totally shocked."

<*I was not shocked,*> Bob insisted.

Priscilla shot a disbelieving look at the overhead before turning her gaze back to Amanda. "Well, either way, glad to have you aboard, miss…?"

"Call me Amanda, or Mandy, or Red, whatever works," she answered, with a smile.

Tanis coughed and leant in close. "Careful, reading minds is kind of illegal here. I'd keep that ability to yourself."

Priscilla seemed unfazed, but Amanda looked back at her with a look of surprise. "Oh, really? How the hell is that a law if there's no magic here?"

<*You don't need magic to read minds,*> Angela said in a matter-of-fact tone.

"Oh…" Amanda nodded slowly "Umm, anyway…what's the purpose of you joining minds?"

Priscilla smiled, looking pleased to be back on familiar ground. "Well, I'm sure you're aware of how people use avatars—usually non-sentient representations—in virtual reality sims?"

Amanda nodded. "Of course, I love a bit of VR."

"Well, this is the reverse. For Bob, our world and humans are all too simple for him. Manifesting himself to all of us is an onerous task, so he uses avatars."

"Humans as avatars? Curious. I guess it makes sense, though. Are you in there the whole time?"

"No. We work in ninety-day shifts. We need to stay grounded in our humanity so we don't get lost in Bob's mind. We'd be of no use to him, then."

"Is there an ethics issue, with an AI using humans like this?" Amanda asked.

"All the avatars are volunteers and carefully screened. Also, Bob has proven himself to be on our side many times over. It's a mutual choice."

Amanda nodded and looked back at the avatar, but Tanis could also see her eyes studying the bulkheads and overheads, following the paths of things only she could see.

It was slightly disconcerting.

"OK, let's go see the bridge," Tanis suggested as she guided Amanda around to the side passage.

"I hope I wasn't offensive," the redhead said as they approached the bridge's doors.

<*I had money on you saying something dumb,*> Angela said with a laugh. <*You cost me…well, nothing, because I don't need money.*>

"Well, as long as I'm amusing you," Amanda replied with a raised eyebrow.

"You were fine," Tanis replied. "She gets that a lot. It's too bad Amavia wasn't here to meet you. She used to be an avatar as well, but now she doesn't qualify."

Amanda turned to face Tanis. "Oh really? Wow…she really didn't explain what her old job was very well."

"Crap!" Tanis exclaimed. "In all the excitement, I forgot that you were at Virginis! What ended up happening there? Is everyone OK?"

Partway through Amanda's recitation of the prior two days' events, Tanis led her into the nearby conference room, where the admiral leant against the table, almost slack-jawed as she listened to the tale of a magical battle aboard Cerka Station and *Sabrina*.

At the end, all she could manage to say was, "Stars."

<OK…next time there's a magic fight, we need to be in on it, Amanda,> Angela admonished. *<Seriously, that sounds amazing.>*

"Intense, more like," she admitted. "Though now that we know that your stasis shields can trap a Magus, you'll have a good defensive weapon against them. I couldn't even Port through Bob's. Only when he flickered it to communicate with me could I get out, and that was really tricky."

"Good to know," Tanis said quietly. "I can't wait to read Jessica's report on that attack. Should be a wild one."

"It's a great crew you have there. That's one hell of a ship."

"You got that right," she agreed. "OK, let's show you the rest of this one. We can work our way down to my place—we're having a bit of a celebration that I should get back to eventually."

Amanda seemed suitably impressed by the bridge, commenting at one point that it was significantly larger than the one on her ship, the *Arkady*.

From there, they took a maglev to the Prairie Park, with Amanda exclaiming how it was beyond surreal to be on a starship so big it had train stations.

A few minutes later, they were strolling through the park when a soft cough came from the branches of a nearby tree.

"Ooooh, look, a cougar," Amanda exclaimed.

"Uh huh," Tanis replied. "He's the alpha. Going on almost two hundred years old now. He and I have seen a lot."

Amanda smirked.

"What's funny?" Tanis asked.

"I have a cat of my own, a saber-tooth called Samhain. He's my familiar. At a little over eight hundred years old, he's getting grumpy in his old age."

Tanis blinked at her. "Just how old are you?"

"One thousand, two hundred, and ninety years old, give or

take a few months."

"Well, you look good for it," Tanis said with a smile.

"Thanks. This is lovely, though," Amanda said, waving at the scenery around her. "A bit of greenery, it's nice. I'm a country girl at heart. Grew up in the Irish countryside, you know?"

"Glad you like it, but this is nothing. Just wait…"

Amanda gave her a curious look, as if wondering what secrets she was keeping from her.

"Well, I've not seen a warship with wildlife on it before," she mused. "It seems more like a pleasure craft or a museum than a capital ship."

"That would have been its ultimate destiny, if this war hadn't landed on our doorstep."

Amanda nodded. "I know that tale."

Eventually, they reached the maglev line that would take them to the port habitation cylinder, which Tanis informed Amanda was named Ol' Sam.

"Now that is awesome. You've got a feckin' planet inside your spaceship," the Magus enthused in a jovial tone as she gazed at the rolling hills that wrapped around the habitation cylinder. "I've not been inside one of these before. Shite, look at that…there's a lake above our heads!"

"Just a small one," Tanis qualified.

"Heh, love it," Amanda commented.

Tanis took the woman's hand and led her off the maglev platform and into the forest that surrounded her lakehouse.

"C'mon. Joe will love to meet you, as will my daughters. You're going to have to do a bit of magic for them, though."

"Like you have to twist my arm for that!"

DEPARTURE

STELLAR DATE: 06.02.8948 (Adjusted Years)

LOCATION: ISS *I2*, Ol' Sam

REGION: Carthage, New Canaan System

"Well," Amanda said wistfully. "I would love to stay a little longer, but I have stuff to do in my own universe."

The pair stood at the end of the dock that led out into the lake outside of Tanis's house, a gentle breeze picking at the Magus's crimson hair.

"I understand," Tanis replied. "I have a queue of messages as long as this ship."

<*And I'm tired of playing your secretary,*> Angela added.

"Your family is beautiful, Blondie. You keep them safe, you hear? Or you'll have me to answer to," Amanda said, her tone light and humorous.

Tanis smiled back. "I will."

"Well, with all the weirdness back home, I didn't think I'd see anything new over here, but you guys have officially surprised me."

"We're a 'go big, or go home' sort of people. Well, now that we have a home, at least."

"Home's important," Amanda agreed, thinking of her own little corner of her universe.

An idea occurred to her as she gazed out over the picturesque landscape of Ol' Sam. Her mind went to BOB's Bar, and then to Inisfail, her pocket spirit realm back on Earth.

I wonder if Void can move Inisfail out of my universe? she thought. *Maybe then I can access it from anywhere.*

"You shifting out of this universe already?" Tanis asked, poking fun at her.

"Hmmm? Oh, no, sorry, just lost in thought about home."

Tanis nodded in understanding.

"Maybe when you're done with your war," Amanda continued, "and I'm done chasing these Reavers across multiple universes, we can meet up again and really relax."

"I know the perfect place," Tanis said.

"Until then, I'm going to leave you with a little gift," Amanda said with a coy smile, turning to face her friend.

~Bob? I'm going to Port my ship aboard as a present for Tanis. Can you show me where would be a good spot?~

<Of course.>

The AI provided an image of a large docking bay, and then a larger image of the ship with her position and the bay highlighted.

~Thanks. I'm going to miss those dulcet tones of yours.~

<*Indeed,*> Bob replied, his tone that of an exasperated parent.

"A gift?" Tanis asked.

Amanda chuckled and held up a finger. "Hold on," she said as she reached out with her power and shaped the Essentia within her to suit her needs.

With a snap, she Ported them both across the ship and into the allotted docking bay. Simultaneously, she Ported her ship and its contents into the *I2,* causing them all to appear at the same moment.

"Whoa," Tanis said, grabbing Amanda's arm to steady herself as she looked around the room, and then up at the ship before them.

<*That was disorienting,*> Angela muttered.

"For you," Amanda told Tanis, gesturing at the Aether Ship.

"Really?" she asked.

<*Nice ship,*> Angela praised, as the ramp levered open and Jinx walked out.

"Hey, Amanda—oh, hi," Jinx said, looking at Tanis.

"Hi yourself."

"This is Jinx, an AI that Jessica helped. She's returning with me," Amanda explained.

"You're Tanis, right?" Jinx asked. "And Angela?"

"I am. It's a pleasure to meet you," Tanis said, shaking Jinx's hand.

<*Same for me,*> Angela added.

"Likewise," Jinx returned. "Wow, this is amazing. I've heard so much about you from Sabrina and Iris. I love the ship, by the way… Oooh, is Bob here?"

<*I am,*> Bob answered.

"Bob! I'm a big fan," Jinx effused.

<*Thank you,*> he replied with a rumbling chuckle.

"Are you sure you want to come with me?" Amanda asked.

"Yes, of course. Sorry, I've just heard so much about this ship."

Amanda smiled warmly. "It's okay."

"So, you're leaving this here?" Tanis gestured at the small vessel. "You don't need it to get back home?"

"Nope. It's all yours. Do as you want with it. I only needed it to get here from Virginis. You might need to put some engines in it of your own tech, though."

"I'm sure Earnest will have fun with it," Tanis replied.

Amanda nodded. "Well, it's been a blast, Blondie."

"It's been good to see you again. Looking forward to catching up again sometime," Tanis agreed.

"You can count on it. Come here, give me a hug," Amanda said, pulling her in. Finally separating and stepping back, she gave Tanis one last smile. "See you soon."

With a snap, she and Jinx vanished, appearing once more in Bob's node chamber.

~Sorry, just a quick pit stop,~ Amanda said over a private Link to Jinx.

<*Having trouble leaving our universe?*> Bob asked.

Amanda stepped up to the railing and stared deep into his node.

~She's going to ascend, isn't she?~

Bob didn't reply.

~I can see it. The same energies interacting with her that do with you, just on a lesser scale. I'm right, aren't I?~

<*Perhaps,*> Bob allowed.

Amanda took the lack of denial as affirmation and nodded.

~I thought so,~ she said, her tone serious. *~Watch over her, won't you?~*

<*Always,*> Bob replied.

Amanda inclined her head once more. "I'll be back, one

day," she said aloud, as she summoned her Magic and pushed through the skin of this universe and back into hers.

With a resounding snap of displaced air, Amanda and Jinx appeared back in her universe, on the main deck of the *Arkady*, where it was still docked on Sol Prime.

Amanda breathed a sigh of relief and walked over to the nearby couch, perching on the edge of it as she took a few more deep breaths.

"That crossing took a lot out of you, didn't it," Jinx said.

Amanda nodded. "They're exhausting, but it's good to be back."

"So, is this your ship? The *Arkady*?"

"Yup. Certainly is. It's your home now as well, if you'd like."

"Are you sure?"

"I mean, I don't know what your plans are, but the offer is there. You're free to do what you like. It's up to you, really."

"I was planning to stay with you, if that's acceptable."

Amanda smiled, feeling relieved.

If she were being honest with herself, she had felt a little worried about the idea of Jinx gallivanting around an unfamiliar universe, and would probably have tried to persuade her to stay anyway.

"Of course," she said, smiling. "Let's find you a room."

"Thank you. I did have an idea though…"

"Oh?" Amanda asked.

"Well, I got along really well with Sabrina, and I liked the setup she had. I was embedded within a computer on a ship before, but that was very different. Sabrina is free. She can travel to stars and use a body to visit stations…. That's what I want."

"You want to be embedded in a ship?"

Jinx nodded. "I do. This ship, if you'll have me."

Amanda smiled, got up, and pulled Jinx into a hug. "I would be honored for you to be the *Arkady*'s AI," she said, pulling away with a warm smile on her face.

"Thank you," Jinx replied. "It's been an interesting couple of days."

"It sure has. Oh, speaking of which…" Amanda said.

She focused on her time sense to see how much had passed between her departure and her return, and found she'd only been gone for a little over a day.

"Huh, interesting," she mused, wondering if other universes would be different.

"Everything okay?" Jinx asked.

"Everything's fine," Amanda replied.

Essentia burst suddenly nearby, and the familiar chrome form of Void appeared out of thin air.

"Shite, woman, you scared me."

"Apologies, Amanda," Void replied. "I wanted to offer my congratulations on a job well done. The Reavers have retreated from that universe. I presume everything went smoothly?"

"Well, I'm not sure about that, but yes, we prevailed. I do have one question, though. While I was there, I found it harder to use Magic, as if it was more of a strain to pull the Essentia to me. Do you know why that would be?"

"Aaaah, yes. This can happen sometimes. Essentia permeates the entire multiverse, but while in some universes it flows freely, such as in ours, in others, it is more limited, making Magic harder. The universes with fewer or no supernatural creatures tend to have less Essentia running through them. It's something to be aware of, but you seem to have handled it well."

"I got there in the end," Amanda nodded. "And it was fun…good to see my friends again."

"Then you will be pleased to know that I have another mission for you," Void said.

THE END

*****

Read on for information about the next Quantum Legends book, and the other series these characters appear in.

AFTERWORD

Thank you for reading this first book in the Quantum Legends Series. This experiment was a lot of fun to write, and I think we have a book that both myself and Michael can be proud of.

I hope you enjoyed reading it as much as we did writing it.

Amanda's multiverse adventures don't stop here. There will be more books in this series to come.

Watch my facebook group to be kept up to date with the latest news: www.facebook.com/groups/MagiSagaFans

In the meantime, you can follow the continuing adventures of Amanda, Jessica, Cheeky and Tanis in their respective series.

Many thanks,
Andrew

* * * * *

I had a fantastic time writing this book with Andrew Dobell, and it was a lot of fun to have these characters meet.

Regarding where this book sits in the Aeon 14 Universe's timeline, it follows the events of A Surreptitious Rescue of Friends and Foes, in the Perseus Gate Season 2 series.

If you've not read any Aeon 14 books, I recommend starting with Destiny Lost, where you'll meet the crew of *Sabrina*, though with a different captain.

Thanks,
Michael Cooper

BOOKS BY ANDREW DOBELL

Star Magi Saga – Space Fantasy

Star Magi – Book 1

Magi Nexus – Book 2

War Magi – Book 3

Star Magi Saga Tales – Space Fantasy

Maiden Voyage – Prequel

Epiphany – Book 2

Quantum Legends

Anomaly on Cerka

The Magi Saga – Urban Fantasy

Magi Dawn: The Magi Saga Book 1

Magi Rising: The Magi Saga Book 2

Magi Omen: The Magi Saga Book 3

Magi Edge: The Magi Saga Book 4

Magi Odyssey: The Magi Saga Book 5

Magi Descent: The Magi Saga book 6

Magi Rebirth: The Magi Saga book 7

Tales of the Magi Saga – Urban Fantasy

Angel of Tarut

His Love

Hack Imperfect

Casino Red

Uprising

A Thoroughly Modern Witch

Pilgrimage

Wasteland Road Knights – Post Apocalyptic

Liberation

Exploration

Revelation

Determination

The New Prometheus - Cyberpunk

The New Prometheus

The Prometheus Gambit

The Prometheus Trap

Prometheus Vengeance

Anthologies I am part of:

The Expanding Universe – Sci-Fi

The Expanding Universe 3 – Sci-Fi

Pew Pew – A fist full of Pews

Bobs Bar 1

Bobs Bar 2

Sign up to my Mailing List.

www.andrewdobellauthor.co.uk

THE BOOKS OF AEON 14

Keep up to date with what is releasing in Aeon 14 with the free Aeon 14 Reading Guide.

The Sentience Wars: Origins (Age of the Sentience Wars – w/James S. Aaron)
- Books 1-3 Omnibus: Lyssa's Rise

- Book 1: Lyssa's Dream
- Book 2: Lyssa's Run
- Book 3: Lyssa's Flight
- Book 4: Lyssa's Call
- Book 5: Lyssa's Flame

Legends of the Sentience Wars (Age of the Sentience Wars – w/James S. Aaron)
- Volume 1: The Proteus Bridge
- Volume 2: Vesta Burning

The Sentience Wars: Solar War 1 (Age of the Sentience Wars – w/James S. Aaron)
- Book 1: Eve of Destruction

Enfield Genesis (Age of the Sentience Wars – w/Lisa Richman)
- Book 1: Alpha Centauri
- Book 2: Proxima Centauri
- Book 3: Tau Ceti
- Book 4: Epsilon Eridani
- Book 5: Sirius (April 2019)

Origins of Destiny (The Age of Terra)
- Prequel: Storming the Norse Wind
- Prequel: Angel's Rise: The Huntress (available on Patreon)
- Book 1: Tanis Richards: Shore Leave
- Book 2: Tanis Richards: Masquerade

- Book 3: Tanis Richards: Blackest Night
- Book 4: Tanis Richards: Kill Shot

The Intrepid Saga (The Age of Terra)
- Book 1: Outsystem
- Book 2: A Path in the Darkness
- Book 3: Building Victoria

- The Intrepid Saga Omnibus – *Also contains Destiny Lost, book 1 of the Orion War series*

- Destiny Rising – *Special Author's Extended Edition comprised of both Outsystem and A Path in the Darkness with over 100 pages of new content.*

The Warlord (Before the Age of the Orion War)
- Books 1-3 Omnibus: The Warlord of Midditerra

- Book 1: The Woman Without a World
- Book 2: The Woman Who Seized an Empire
- Book 3: The Woman Who Lost Everything

The Orion War
- Books 1-3 Omnibus (includes Ignite the Stars anthology)

- Book 1: Destiny Lost
- Book 2: New Canaan
- Book 3: Orion Rising
- Book 4: The Scipio Alliance
- Book 5: Attack on Thebes
- Book 6: War on a Thousand Fronts
- Book 7: Precipice of Darkness
- Book 8: Airtha Ascendancy
- Book 9: The Orion Front
- Book 10: Starfire (2019)
- Book 11: Race Across Spacetime (2019)
- Book 12: Return to Sol (2019)

Building New Canaan (Age of the Orion War – w/J.J. Green)
- Book 1: Carthage
- Book 2: Tyre
- Book 3: Troy
- Book 4: Athens

Tales of the Orion War
- Book 1: Set the Galaxy on Fire
- Book 2: Ignite the Stars
- Book 3: Burn the Galaxy to Ash (2019)

Perilous Alliance (Age of the Orion War – w/Chris J. Pike)
- Book 1-3 Omnibus: Crisis in Silstrand

- Book 1: Close Proximity
- Book 2: Strike Vector
- Book 3: Collision Course
- Book 4: Impact Imminent
- Book 5: Critical Inertia
- Book 6: Impulse Shock

Rika's Marauders (Age of the Orion War)
- Book 1-3 Omnibus: Rika Activated

- Prequel: Rika Mechanized
- Book 1: Rika Outcast
- Book 2: Rika Redeemed
- Book 3: Rika Triumphant
- Book 4: Rika Commander
- Book 5: Rika Infiltrator
- Book 6: Rika Unleashed
- Book 7: Rika Conqueror

Non-Aeon 14 Anthologies containing Rika stories
- Bob's Bar Volume 2
- Backblast Area Clear

The Genevian Queen (Age of the Orion War)

- Book 1: Rika Rising (2019)
- Book 2: Rika Coronated (2019)
- Book 3: Rika Reigns (2019)

Perseus Gate (Age of the Orion War)
Season 1: Orion Space
- Episode 1: The Gate at the Grey Wolf Star
- Episode 2: The World at the Edge of Space
- Episode 3: The Dance on the Moons of Serenity
- Episode 4: The Last Bastion of Star City
- Episode 5: The Toll Road Between the Stars
- Episode 6: The Final Stroll on Perseus's Arm
- Eps 1-3 Omnibus: The Trail Through the Stars
- Eps 4-6 Omnibus: The Path Amongst the Clouds

Season 2: Inner Stars
- Episode 1: A Meeting of Bodies and Minds
- Episode 2: A Deception and a Promise Kept
- Episode 3: A Surreptitious Rescue of Friends and Foes
- Episode 4: A Victory and a Crushing Defeat
- Episode 5: A Trial and the Tribulations (2019)
- Episode 6: A Deal and a True Story Told (2019)
- Episode 7: A New Empire and An Old Ally (2019)
- Eps 1-3 Omnibus: A Siege and a Salvation from Enemies

Hand's Assassin (Age of the Orion War – w/T.G. Ayer)
- Book 1: Death Dealer
- Book 2: Death Mark (2019)

Machete System Bounty Hunter (Age of the Orion War – w/Zen DiPietro)
- Book 1: Hired Gun
- Book 2: Gunning for Trouble
- Book 3: With Guns Blazing

Fennington Station Murder Mysteries (Age of the Orion War)
- Book 1: Whole Latte Death (w/Chris J. Pike)
- Book 2: Cocoa Crush (w/Chris J. Pike)

Vexa Legacy (Age of the FTL Wars – w/Andrew Gates)
- Book 1: Seas of the Red Star

The Empire (Age of the Orion War)
- Book 1: The Empress and the Ambassador
- Book 2: Consort of the Scorpion Empress (2019)
- Book 3: By the Empress's Command (2019)

The Sol Dissolution (The Age of Terra)
- Book 1: Venusian Uprising (2019)
- Book 2: Scattered Disk (2019)
- Book 3: Jovian Offensive (2019)
- Book 4: Fall of Terra (2019)

ABOUT THE AUTHORS

Andrew has always been something of a storyteller and a creative. As a child, he dreamed of becoming a comic book artist. While that dream never really came true, it did develop into a love of telling stories through RPGs like Dungeons and Dragons and Vampire the Masquerade.

Having always been an artist, spending time as a freelance illustrator and wedding photographer, Andrew now splits his time a a book cover designer and author.

He lives in Surrey in the UK with his wife, three boys, dog and cat.

www.andrewdobellauthor.co.uk

* * * * *

Michael Cooper likes to think of himself as a jack-of-all-trades (and hopes to become master of a few). When not writing, he can be found writing software, working in his shop at his latest carpentry project, or likely reading a book.

He shares his home with a precocious young girl, his wonderful wife (who also writes), two cats, a never-ending list of things he would like to build, and ideas...

Find out what's coming next at www.aeon14.com